Content Notes can be found at the back of the book.

Copyright © 2025 by Radar DeBoard

All rights reserved.

No part of this publication may be reproduced, distributed, or transmitted in any form or by any means, including photocopying, recording, or other electronic or mechanical methods, without the prior written permissions of the publisher, except as permitted by U.S. copyright law. For permission requests, contact trubornpress@gmail.com

The story, all names, characters, and incidents portrayed in this production are fictitious. No identification with actual persons (living or deceased), places, buildings, and products is intended or should be inferred.

Published by Truborn Press

Edited by Tasha Reynolds

Cover Design by Matt Seff Barnes

Interior Design by Truborn Design

ISBN 979-8-9915969-7-8 (Paperback)

FIRST EDITION

10 9 8 7 6 5 4 3 2 1

Disclaimer: Unauthorized Sharing or Use of Digital Copies

This digital content is protected by copyright law. Please note the following:

• Do not share, distribute, or sell this digital content, in whole or in part, without the express written consent of the copyright owner.

• Do not upload any portion of this content to any AI generator, platform, or system without authorization.

• Unauthorized use, reproduction, or distribution of this content may result in civil and/or criminal penalties. Support creators by respecting their intellectual property.

THE VIOLET GLOW OF THE DAYTENS

RADAR DEBOARD

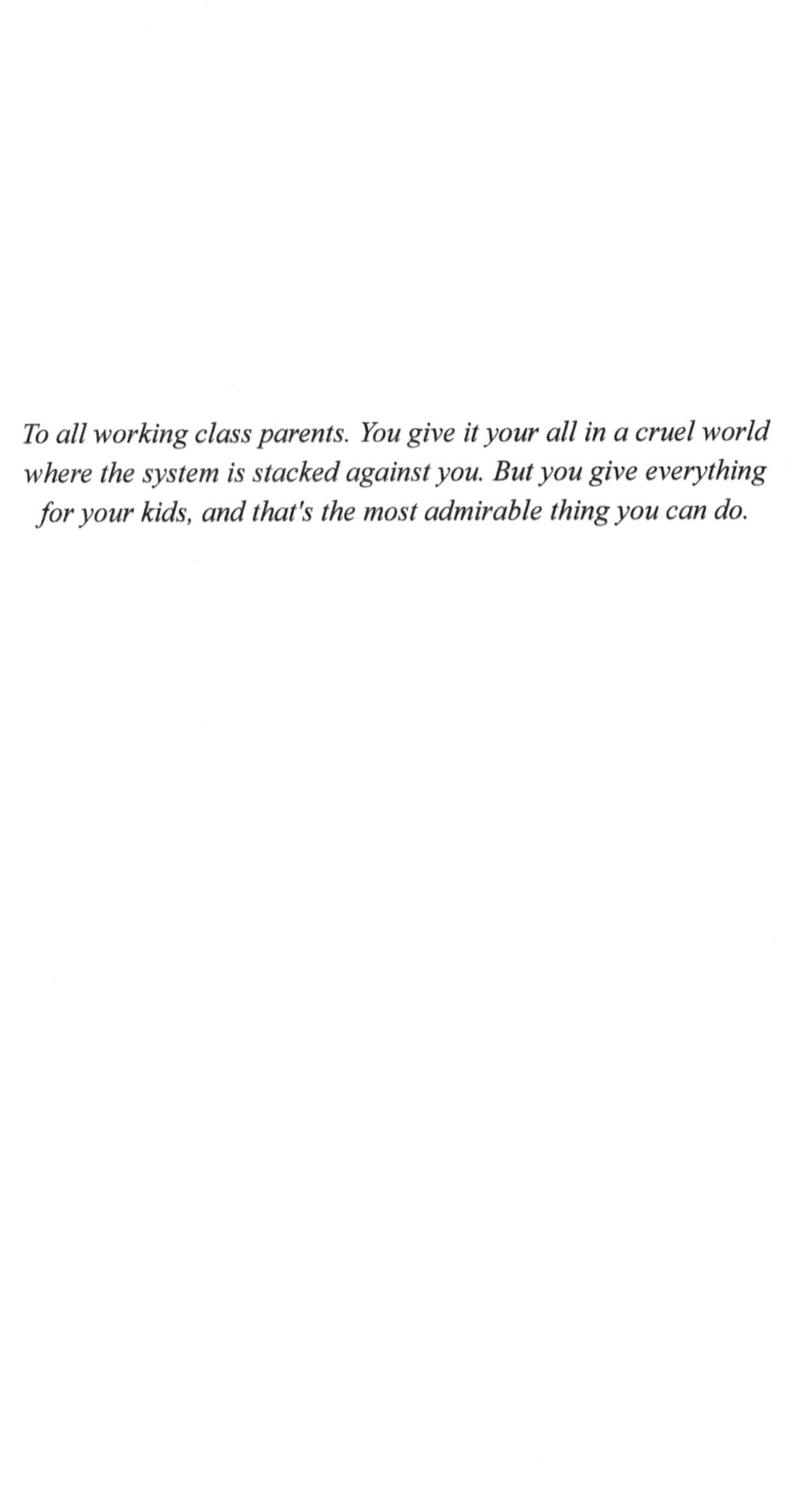

To all working class parents. You give it your all in a cruel world where the system is stacked against you. But you give everything for your kids, and that's the most admirable thing you can do.

THE VIOLET GLOW OF THE DAYTENS

RADAR DEBOARD

ONE

IT'S THE OLD HAG'S TIME

The sound of dozens of individual pops broke through the silence as the sole inhabitant of the decaying house tried to stand. More noises emanated from the ancient knees as they struggled to bear the thin frame of the elderly woman. Grunts began to escape from the lips of the senior citizen as her efforts only lifted her up inch by inch. Finally, she came as close as her body possibly could to fully standing. It had been over two decades since she had been able to fully straighten her back, so she was forced to walk about in a hunched position. That meant she had to lift her head ever so slightly to properly see what was in front of her, which was a sizable task considering her age.

Once firmly on her feet, the weathered woman took in a series of winded breaths and steadied herself by resting a shaking hand on the back of a nearby chair. She took a minute or so, then began an excruciatingly slow walk toward the bathroom that lay a good twenty feet away. Each step was a monumental task as her near-nonexistent muscles strained, and ligaments throughout her legs grew dangerously close to ripping. Of course, there was also pain. Pain from bone scraping against bone, as there was next to no cartilage left in her body. Her muscles screamed in agony, as any small amount of movement overexerted them. Above all though, a constant, dull ache radiated amongst all her organs.

The only time she wasn't in constant misery was when she remained completely still, which happened to be exactly how she lived her life: an almost motionless existence that was only disrupted when she needed to use the restroom. There were no TVs in her house for entertainment; she grew up in a time before those and never really liked them. She kept no devices in the house to play music, nor did she own any books. Her days were spent sitting completely still in a chair, staring into space. Many would say that wasn't a life at all, but she would. She was alive, and that was the most important thing to her. Above all, she valued her life more than anything else.

That had been her mindset for decades, and it was the driving factor that led to her minimal existence. This way of thinking had steered her to gradually abandon all the additional niceties that life could offer. She did not leave the house except for the rare instances she needed food. There was no feasible form of entertainment or way to elicit enjoyment within the four walls of her living space. No pictures adorned the walls, as they were left bare. Besides a well-worn bed and chair that had been purchased decades prior, no other furniture was present. Even the kitchen was bare, apart from the canned food that she ate exclusively and several can openers that she used to access her sole source of sustenance.

Perhaps the most striking absence of all though, was the complete lack of companionship. There hadn't been a single conversation within the walls of the house in over twenty years. No one came to visit, and she never interacted with anyone unless it was absolutely necessary. This meant that on average she muttered less than a hundred words in a year. She was all alone, completely by design. Her life was immersed in silence, and she enjoyed it that way. To her, sitting in utter stillness with only the sounds of her breathing was more than enough to sustain oneself. There was but one thing she had any envy for, and that was youth. More specifically, the youth of those with perfectly functioning bodies, who did not spend their waking hours trying to keep agony at bay. That was the sole thing she was envious of.

With hindsight and her old age, she realized that she had wasted her youth. She had been a housewife, a mother, and the equivalent of a second-class citizen for most of her body's vigorous years. The amount of her life wasted on menial and pointless tasks she had undertaken as a good wife made her sick just thinking about them. Literal years had been thrown away to raise a group of snot-nosed brats and please a husband who didn't even try to reciprocate her efforts. By the time she reclaimed her freedom, her vessel was well past its prime. At that point, her flesh had begun to degrade, and so her focus turned to simply staying alive as long as possible.

In all regards, she had accomplished her goal, as she was far older than the average life expectancy. She had outlived her daughter and even her granddaughter. The old hag had survived for over a century, growing more secluded and crotchety with each passing year. Long ago she had made her survival the top priority, and she had succeeded. It took blocking out everything else, but she had managed to do it. Her unbending focus also had an unintended consequence as well; it dulled every emotion except for one, anger. Rage had become her only friend, growing to the point where even a small creaking noise breaking the silence of her home sent her into an irate rant.

The anger and hatred were fine with her; in fact, she leaned into it. Amplifying those emotions made it so much easier to dull the others that she deemed negative to her survival. Joy, sadness, compassion; all were just feelings that were holding her back. However, the one she viewed as the greatest enemy of her survival was fear. Above all else, she believed fear would make her weak and susceptible to death. This was why she had put most of her attention toward conquering it, and after years of effort, she finally succeeded. There was nothing that made her veins run cold with terror, as she truly believed she could not be threatened. Death had no hold over her thanks to her drive and some additional help from an outside force far greater in power than any human.

Despite all her accomplishments in driving out the vestiges of her humanity, she still hadn't been able to eliminate the need to evacuate waste from her body. Hence why she occasionally had to struggle her way down the hall to the lone bathroom in her house. Most of the time it would take roughly five minutes for her to simply reach the facilities, and this instance was no different. In fact, she was moving slightly slower than usual as radiating waves of pain had begun to assail her knees. Instead of lingering on the pain, she turned her thoughts toward the frustration she felt from her body not working as well as it used to. This brought forth an intense rage for her situation, which in turn gave her the drive to push her weak limbs the rest of the way to her goal.

She stumbled through the open door, nearly toppling over onto the floor, but managed to catch herself on the sink. Her arms shook with exertion as it took every ounce of strength to keep from crumbling into a heap. The physical test brought sweat dripping down her ancient and wrinkled cheeks while her breathing was extremely labored. Finally, she managed to right her legs underneath her and was able to properly stand, though she still supported herself against the sink. She held herself there, gradually raising her gaze to glance at herself in the filthy mirror. Like the rest of the house, the reflective surface hadn't been cleaned in years, but she could still identify herself through the caked-on layers of dust. The dull eyes and decrepit visage that stared back at her filled her with disgust.

She wanted to turn away, but something caught her attention around the area of her chest. Her gaze drifted down her reflected body to find that, right around her sternum, a strange phenomenon was occurring. It was nearly imperceptible to her eyes, but she was just able to pick up on an incredibly faint, purplish glow.

"I… I don't understand," her hoarse voice barely managed to croak out as she stared at the unnatural light emanating from her sternum.

As the seconds ticked by, the dull glow began to grow in intensity to the point where it was easily visible. The hag's hands violently trembled, but not from exertion as they had before. That violet color brought on something she had not experienced in a long time, fear, and it was rapidly eating away at her. A true sensation of dread pulsated through her being, causing her gut to tighten while also overwhelming her mind. The glow brightened further and deep within it; the silhouette of the decrepit woman's beating heart appeared.

An audible wheeze escaped from her lungs as terror swirled about, constricting the surroundings in on her. Engulfed by the horror of the situation, her bladder released itself, sending a warm stream of piss pouring down the inside of her left leg. She didn't notice the urine, as her skin was numb thanks to the adrenaline coursing through her veins.

"This can't be happening!" she cried out in a raspy wail.

Gifted with a newfound strength from the fear, she managed to flee from the bathroom and into the hallway. She stumbled down the corridor, hugging the wall to keep her body from falling and colliding with the ground. The terror continued to squeeze on her organs, now moving its way back up her body.

In desperation, she called out, "You can't do this! Not to me!"

She nearly lost her footing but managed to recover by slamming against the wall. The fear was making up for lost time, completely engulfing her, pressing itself down onto every part of her.

Once again, she cried out, "I've done everything for this! Everything! I have taken all your gifts. You can't do this to me!"

Sharp pain stung her chest as the feeling of terror finally reached the area around her sternum. Unrelenting pressure flattened against her heart, causing an irregular rhythm. Acting in instinct, one of her hands left the wall and desperately grasped at the spot that was riddled with agony. Another wave of pressure forced itself down onto the organ, and her heartbeat stopped for a second. That was enough to throw off her next step and her toes caught on the carpet. As her body careened toward the floor, the final push of terror slammed against her heart and the organ ceased beating altogether. By the time her face connected with the carpet, she was dead. Her body lay there, completely motionless as silence once again settled over the house. Silence, just how she had liked it.

TWO

NO TEARS FOR A MATRIARCH

A nudge broke Jenelle from the light nap she had been taking. She looked over to see her mother glancing at her out of the corner of one eye. Groggy and somewhat annoyed that she had been awakened, she rubbed the sides of her head while sitting fully up in her seat.

"What?" she asked with a grumpy tone.

"Did you have a good nap?" her mother joked as she took a slow turn onto a dirt road. The inside of the car shifted a bit as it adjusted to the change in terrain. Laurie waited a few moments to get acclimated to the new conditions before taking another playful jab at her daughter. "I thought you were too old for those."

Jenelle rolled her eyes. "Not when I'm bored out of my mind." She turned her gaze to the passenger window and stared at the open fields with nothing in them for miles.

The older woman sighed, knowing exactly what her daughter meant. "I know it's not much to look at."

"It's *nothing* to look at," Jenelle jumped in to correct her mom.

"Okay … there's nothing to look at, but it's not that bad, trust me. You only have to put up with it for a couple of hours, but I had to live with it."

Jenelle turned to look at her mom. "Well, I can see why you got the hell out of here."

"Hey, hey, language!" Laurie scolded her before flashing a smile. "But you're right, I'm glad I don't live around here anymore." She slowly shook her head as she thought back on some teenage memories. "There was never anything fun going on around here unless you were willing to do a few illegal things."

That got Jenelle's attention, and she perked up. "Oh really? What kind of illegal things?"

Laurie chuckled, "Oh … standard stuff really. Some egging here and there, setting off the occasional firework." She paused to glance at her daughter with a wry smile as she added, "Perhaps some drinking was involved on an occasion or two."

"Mom! No way!" Jenelle gasped, completely shocked at the revelation. Seeing an opportunity, she hoped to blindside her mom by suddenly asking, "Does that mean I can drink?"

Without missing a beat, her mother sharply replied, "Absolutely not!"

"Aww, come on! That's not fair. You just admitted that you were drinking at my age."

Laurie pointed a finger at Jenelle as she replied, "Ah! I never said how old I was. Nice try though."

"Come on," Jenelle pleaded, "just a bottle of wine. Dad will never find out." When she was met by a knowing glance, she let out a defeated groan. She grumbled, "It's the least you could do for dragging me out here."

"I'm sorry I've ruined your weekend and brought an end to your entire social existence!" Laurie said in over-the-top exaggeration. She glanced over to see the angry look on her child's face and added, "I think you'll survive. Plus, I don't want to be out here either kiddo, but we have to."

"But why?" Jenelle moaned. "It doesn't make any sense. I never even met this lady. Why do I have to help clean out her home and get covered in old person smell?"

"Because I said so," Laurie replied, somewhat annoyed by her daughter's whining.

They traveled down the dirt road in silence for several minutes until finally coming up to a janky-looking crossroads. Laurie took a right and broke the silence. "We have to do this because there's no one else to. We are the only family your great-great-grandmother had left."

"How come we never visited her, then?" Jenelle inquired with a snooty tone.

"Well … for starters," Laurie gestured at the road, "this drive is an absolute nightmare. But more importantly … she was downright mean."

Jenelle, annoyed by the watered-down language her mother used, bluntly asked, "You mean she was a bitch?"

Immediately, she regretted saying that and waited for her mother to give her a good verbal thrashing for using such language. To Jenelle's surprise, her mom responded in agreement, "Yeah, she was a bitch."

This was absolutely shocking for her, not only because her mother never cussed, but because Laurie also firmly believed that one should never speak ill of the dead. That meant that this lady, this distant relative, must have been truly unbearable.

"Woah … I can't believe you actually said 'bitch'."

Laurie shot her daughter a glance as she responded, "Well don't tell your father." She quickly added, "And don't think you can start saying it now either. This is just a one-time thing because of how truly awful your great-great-grandmother was."

"Was she really that bad?" Jenelle asked with a healthy dose of skepticism and intrigue in her voice.

"It wasn't just one thing," Laurie replied. She noticed the confused look on her daughter's face and clarified, "She didn't do one or two things that made you hate her, she was just unpleasant to be around. There was no off switch with her, she was constantly and only mean. Nothing, and I mean nothing, that came out of that woman's mouth was ever nice."

Jenelle was not very satisfied with that answer and prodded, "But what did she do that was so bad?"

Laurie let out a long sigh. "I only met her once. Just once, but that was enough. I was eight or nine at the time, I think. By that point she was already eighty … maybe even eighty-five or somewhere around there." She paused to slow down and carefully turn onto a much narrower road. "Anyway, there was a family reunion of sorts going on, so all my aunts and uncles and cousins were there. We were having the gathering at the local church because it was the only building big enough to fit more than twenty people in it at once. I remember as clear as day how everyone was having a good time, talking and playing about … and how all that happiness got sucked out of the room the second she stepped inside it."

"What do you mean? Like everyone stopped talking just 'cause she showed up?"

"Exactly," Laurie said with a nod. "All the grownups immediately fell silent, though us kids kept playing until she screamed at the top of her lungs for someone to 'shut those damn kids up'." She shuddered. "Her voice was so raspy. It sounded like she had gargled sandpaper. Yuck! I think that voice is going to haunt me for the rest of my life. Anywho, she shuffles her way over to the first available chair and plops down in it, then immediately starts shouting out orders. I remember all the grownups started running about like chickens with their heads cut off just trying to please this ugly-looking witch."

"Why did they do it?" Jenelle asked. "I mean, why not ignore her?"

Laurie shrugged. "I honestly have no idea. Maybe it was because she was the matriarch of the family, or maybe they were just raised to respect their elders … which she certainly was. I can't tell you why, but they just did." She thought about the question for a moment then commented, "She did have this … this presence … I guess you'd call it. When she was in the room, there was this unsettling feeling. It just hung in the air. A really bad vibe that didn't feel natural. I don't know how to explain it, but it felt like there was something bad, something unnatural following her around. And if you didn't listen to her …"

"What? What would happen?" Jenelle eagerly asked after her mother had trailed off.

"Honestly, probably nothing," Laurie replied as they turned yet again onto a dirt path that led to a lone house. As they moved over the bumpy terrain she stated, "Welp, we're here, so I think that's that on me recounting some traumatizing childhood memories."

Jenelle rolled her eyes, trying to hide the fact that she was annoyed that she wouldn't be able to find out more about how horrible of a person her distant relative had been. As they drew closer to the house, the details of the dilapidated building became more apparent. It looked like it would topple over at any moment, especially if two people ventured inside it.

"Do we have to go in there?" Jenelle anxiously asked as they came to a stop.

Laurie let out a chuckle. "Yes. We can't clean everything out if we don't go inside, remember?"

"But why do we have to clean it?" she called out to her mother as they exited the car. "This place is in the middle of nowhere. It's not like anyone is going to see it."

Laurie withdrew the keychain from her pocket as they stepped onto the dilapidated, wooden porch. The boards groaned beneath their feet, barely able to support the small amount of weight thrust upon them. "That's where you're wrong," she responded just as she found the right key to use. "I actually managed to sell this place to a guy who flips houses for a living.

His one major stipulation before we handed the place over to him was that we had to clean it out."

The door creaked and moaned as it was lightly pushed open. Before either woman could enter the house, they were both assailed by the putrid stench that shot forth. Jenelle stumbled back from the door and nearly barfed off the edge of the porch. Her mother tried to keep her composure but ended up gagging while pulling her shirt over her nose and pinching her nostrils.

"Oh god! Please don't make me go in there!" Jenelle begged.

Laurie raced back to the car and dug around in the back seat to retrieve a can of air spray. She stood in the doorway, pumping the fresh linen-scented aerosol into the house from a safe distance away. After several minutes of nonstop spray, she finally lowered the can and stepped inside. She took a very cautious whiff of the air and found it to be passable, though some unpleasant hint of the rotten odor continued to linger.

"Okay, it's good to come in now," Laurie called out to her daughter.

Jenelle took a step toward the open door but didn't cross its threshold right away. She hesitated outside, taking a few tentative sniffs, then finally stepped inside. "Why the hell does it smell so bad in here? This isn't regular old people smell. It's so much worse."

"That's because your great-great-grandmother was a hermit," Laurie answered as she scanned the nearly empty living room. The once grey carpet had taken on a clear brownish hue that would need cleaning, but not right away. "So, when she died, it was a while before anyone went looking for her."

"Ugh! So she died here? That's gross," Jenelle shuddered in disgust.

"Yup, you're not wrong," Laurie replied as she made her way across the room and over to the entrance of the kitchen. "The coroner may have picked up the body, but they sure didn't do anything about the smell, so we'll have to do that ourselves."

"That's just fucking great," Jenelle mumbled under her breath while her mother started opening the weathered cabinets in the kitchen.

She glanced at the carpet of the living room while listening to the sounds of wooden cabinets being rifled through. In the back corner of the room, she noticed a distinct spot with a strange color that contrasted against the rest of the carpet. She slowly moved towards it then stopped when she realized the horrific odor that permeated the house was coming from that spot.

"Hey," Laurie called out, "while I'm cleaning out the kitchen, go around the rest of the house and see if there's anything big we need to take care of."

Jenelle glanced at the hallway that lay behind the disgusting blotch on the carpet where her great-great-grandmother had no doubt died, and groaned. She plugged her nose and then quickly raced around the spot and down the hallway. After getting a good ten feet of distance between her and the enormous death stain, she came to a stop at the first door that she saw. The door was open so all she had to do was peer inside to find a bare bathroom with yellowing paint covering the wall. Wanting to spend as little time in there as possible, she quickly opened the drawers under the bathroom sink, finding them to be empty, while also taking note that there was no toothbrush to be found.

She didn't dwell on the dental hygiene of her deceased family member and instead moved back out into the hallway. Jenelle scanned another room, finding it to be empty as well, before coming to a stop at the lone closed door in the house. With a brief bit of hesitation, she turned the knob and allowed the rusted, metal hinges to creak loudly. The door groaned as she gently pushed it out of her way and entered the master bedroom, where a rancid mattress sat atop a rusted, metal bedframe. She was about to turn and leave, assuming there was nothing else in the room, when something caught her attention out of the corner of her eye. There was a small pause in her movements before she crossed the filthy carpet to the lone item placed several feet from the bed.

To her surprise, it was a brown leather book that seemed to be in better condition than anything else in the house. Driven by curiosity, she bent down and picked up the mysterious tome. Immediately, a cold shiver ran down her spine as the sensation of being watched caused the hair on her arms to rise in alarm. Tentatively, she peeked over her shoulder at the open doorway, half expecting someone to be there, but thankfully there wasn't. She let out a sigh of relief, then turned her attention back to the strange book. Upon opening it and flipping through a few pages she found it to be a diary, no doubt belonging to her great-great-grandmother. She scanned some of the cursive writing on a page and frowned. The words that crossed in front of her eyes gave her pause. They described horrific acts, things that if they were true would make her distant relative a killer. But they couldn't possibly be true … could they? The sound of footsteps moving down the hallway drew her attention away from the diary, and instinctively, she hid it behind her back.

"How's it going?" her mother asked as she poked her head into the room.

Jenelle pointed at the bed. "This is all that's here." She felt a twinge of guilt for not mentioning the diary.

"Awesome, this will be easier than I thought," her mom replied with a smile. "Come help me clean up the kitchen then. There's a buttload of cans in there and I need help hauling them out of here."

Jenelle nodded and waited for her mother to move down the hallway before slipping the diary into the waistband of her pants. She would read it later.

THREE
ONE LESS DAYTEN IN THE WORLD

Jenelle struggled to make her way to the park bench as another shooting wave of pain arched across her brain. She had spent decades trying to avoid facing the agony that would come with her death, and now that it was finally there, it was worse than she had imagined. Even though the horrific aches were isolated in her head, the rest of her body was affected by it too. Her movement was sluggish and there were pinpricks of strange sensations coursing throughout her limbs, but those were mostly drowned out by the excruciating pain. She couldn't think of anything except reaching her goal, and that itself was a monumental task.

Eventually, she reached the weathered piece of park property and collapsed onto it. Her back collided with the metal, and caused a jut of pain in her spine that momentarily drew attention away from the agony that was wracking the inside of her head. Jenelle took in gasping breaths of air as fear and panic took hold. She had made the decision to end things, but now that it was actually happening, she was terrified of it. The terror she felt was only natural, an understandable response to the constant torment that assailed her. She didn't know how long this horrible situation was going to last, but she hoped it would end soon enough.

Her silent pleas were answered with a sudden pop that sounded inside her head. The almost incomprehensible pain that had riddled her mind ceased, along with all the feeling in her limbs. She tried to move her arms but found they were paralyzed, locked in place. A few moments passed before she felt the sensation of something warm reaching the top of her lip. The feeling continued as she sat motionless, unable to look to see what the culprit was. Eventually, the warm substance dripped onto her bottom lip and rolled into her mouth. The unique flavor touched her tongue, and she knew immediately that it was blood.

"So … that's how it's going to do it," she barely managed to mutter to herself.

No doubt, she was having an aneurysm or something very similar to it. The bloody nose made it clear that this was a particularly nasty affliction, and that she had minutes, not hours, of life left. She scanned the park as best she could in her paralyzed state and managed to spot a few people scattered about. They were going about their business, paying no attention to the older woman with blood running down her nose. That was fine with Jenelle; even if someone had noticed her predicament, there was nothing that could be done to help. It was better that she left this world without burdening anyone else.

In the end, she was going out on her own terms. Sure, she hadn't chosen how she was going to die, but she had decided for herself that she was ready. Unlike her great-great-grandmother, Jenelle's death wouldn't be filled with fear and terror. That was probably much more than she deserved after all the things she had done. It was honestly a little strange when she thought about it. All the people whom she interacted with throughout her day, whether they be strangers or lifelong friends, didn't know about the horrible secrets she kept … and they never would. There was no evidence of her crimes. The man, no, the *thing*, made sure of that. She would pass out of this world, and no one would ever know how much of a monster she had been.

Another snap sounded inside her head and the salty liquid poured from her nose faster than before. Now that most of the pain was gone, it was honestly a somewhat tranquil way to go. Any remotely peaceful death was certainly too good for her, and she knew it. She wouldn't complain about the relatively easy way out. Her conscience was certainly not happy about the mild exit. There was no justice for those she had hurt, and it looked like there would be no last-minute retribution coming for her. She would die alone on a public bench and that would be the end of it.

"Not too bad of a way to go," she mumbled to herself.

A bit of sunlight peaked out from behind a passing cloud and brought a little heat to the area Jenelle was sitting in. The pleasant warmth washed over her and she gave a weak smile in response. A final pop sounded in her head, and she let out a constrained grunt from her throat as all thoughts were pushed out of her mind. As the life drained from her body, she slumped down until gravity took over and her corpse fell onto its right side. It would be several minutes before anyone took note of her, and it would take longer for someone to place a call to authorities about her body. None of them who saw her corpse understood the importance of her passing. They had no idea that the world had one less monster in it, and it was far better off for it.

FOUR
REVEALED THROUGH A PARTY FOUL

The small kitchen of the apartment could barely hold three people in it, let alone eleven college students. Yet, that was exactly what was happening as the music blasted throughout the small living quarters. It probably wouldn't be long before a noise complaint would be lodged, but no one in the party was thinking about that. Half of them were incredibly inebriated, to the point where they were slurring words, while most of the others were at the very least in no position to drive. Jenelle was hoping to, at the very least, reach a nice buzz, but that was proving to be a little more difficult than she had anticipated. Most of that was because the fridge housed all of the drinks, and it was constantly blocked off by drunk and horny people who had wandered into the kitchen to grab a drink for themselves.

In the two hours she had been there, she had only managed to have two drinks while being pulled into at least six different conversations she wanted no part of. Her average time to make it to and from the fridge was about fifteen minutes, which greatly hindered her opportunities to drink. She hadn't even spotted her friend, Roxy, who was hosting the party. Most likely her friend was out sucking face on the small deck toward the back of the apartment. Jenelle couldn't blame Roxy for getting some at her own party, especially since there were so many people crammed into such a small space. It was quickly getting on her nerves, and by the time she had her third drink in hand, she was debating whether she should just leave. Her mind was made up for her when someone bumped into her as she tried to exit the kitchen. It wasn't very hard, but there was enough force for her to spill her drink on the carpet.

"Are you fucking kidding me?" she tried to shout over the music but the person who had caused the spill didn't even notice her.

She grabbed a few napkins off a nearby table and started rubbing them over the liquor seeping into the carpet. The paper material didn't hold up very well once it got wet, and she ended up just getting bits of napkin stuck in the fabric alongside her fallen beverage. In the middle of her frustration, a pair of dress shoes came into view out of the corner of her eye. The footwear was a clear outlier compared to all the other sneakers and flip-flops she had seen throughout the night. Curious, she brought her focus away from the carpet and up past the dress shoes. Her eyes wander up to find an older man, possibly in his mid-forties, dressed in formal attire that looked like it had come out of the 1920s. There was a solemn expression on the gentleman's face, that combined with his strange attire and his age, rubbed her the wrong way.

"Can I help you?" she asked with a frown. When the strange man did not reply, she raised her voice and a more confrontational tone asked again, "Can I help you?"

"Oh, I'm sorry," came a reply that wasn't from the strange man, but rather someone who was standing next to him.

Jenelle looked at the newcomer, who seemed like he actually belonged at the party. He looked older than her, but only by a few years, most likely in his mid-twenties at the latest.

"I just saw that you spilled your drink and thought you might need some help," the new guy explained.

Jenelle looked back to where the strange man had been standing but found that no one was there. She stared at the empty space in confusion before the new guy waved a hand in front of her face to get her attention.

"You good?" he asked.

"Uhh … yeah, I'm fine," she replied. Jenelle let out a loud sigh. "Well … I still don't have a drink, but whatever."

With a smile that was a little off-putting to Jenelle, the guy responded, "I can fix that! What were you drinking?"

She paused for a few moments, then slowly answered, "Vodka cranberry, but you don't …"

Before she could finish, he had pushed his way into the kitchen. She noticed he was a lot more physical than she had been. He forced his way through the crowd and was at the fridge in a matter of seconds. Jenelle stood, waiting for several minutes by herself until the guy returned with a red, plastic cup in hand.

"Here you go! One vodka cranberry."

"Thanks," she said, while taking the cup. Jenelle took a small sip and glanced around the room. For a brief moment, she thought she had caught sight of the well-dressed weirdo, but there was no one there when she looked again.

"I'm Rourke, by the way," the guy who had gotten her a new drink said.

She turned her attention back to him. With a puzzled look, she repeated, "Rourke?"

"Yeah, that's right. It's a little weird, but if you met my parents you would understand."

Not knowing what to say to that, Jenelle just took another sip of her drink and nodded slowly. Truth be told, she didn't want to be stuck in conversation with this dude. He had been nice in getting her another drink, but there was something … off about him. Plus, she wanted to go home and had no intention of hanging around for much longer.

"So, what do you do?" Rourke asked.

"What do I do?" she repeated as she brought her focus back to Rourke.

She was about to tell him off when an interesting thing caught her eye. There was something off about the guy's nose, but she couldn't put her finger on what it was. The shape of it wasn't weird and its size was normal, yet she was drawn to it. She intently focused on it until she picked up on the faintest glow surrounding it. A strange, violet hue encircled the nose and drew her in. Her mind immediately thought of her great-great-grandmother's diary and how what Jenelle was seeing seemed so similar to what her ancestor had described.

"Um … I guess you don't have to answer that," Rourke said in an annoyed tone, interrupting her focus.

She shook her head and quickly took another sip of her drink so there was a bit more time for her to come up with an explanation for why she had been staring. "Sorry … I was just … uh … trying to remember if I had finished an assignment for one of my classes."

That dumb excuse seemed to work as Rourke's tone changed to one of interest. "Oh, so you're a college student, huh? What school you going to?"

Intrigued by the mysterious violet hue and what it meant, Jenelle decided to stick around for a little bit longer to see if anything else would happen. "I go to Hallowhall."

"Oh cool! They've got a pretty good science department from what I've heard," Rourke replied.

From there he started talking about how he had almost gone there, and how he had several friends who thought the college was nice. None of what he said was of interest to Jenelle; she just kept her attention focused on the faint glow emanating from his nose. She went through a quarter of her drink as he continued to blather on. Several minutes went by before he finally stopped talking long enough for her to ask about him.

"How do you know Roxy?" she inquired.

"Oh, I don't really know her," he admitted. "My friend is her co-worker, and he invited me along for the ride."

"So, you probably don't know anyone here," she inferred.

Rourke smiled, "Well … I like to think I'm getting to know you."

That was a little too creepy for Jenelle's taste. She was about to walk away when she was suddenly hit by a wave of dizziness. Her head felt incredibly heavy, like it was weighing her down while her mind was caught in a haze where she couldn't think clearly. Confusion overtook all her other senses and she stumbled back a bit, bumping into a table.

"Woah, are you okay?" Rourke said as he came close and touched her arm with his hand.

"I'm fine," Jenelle weakly insisted, "I just need some fresh air."

She tried to push past him but the fog covering her mind was getting stronger and she found it difficult to move.

"I think you might need to lie down," Rourke said. He wrapped an arm around her and started to guide her.

"No … I'm fine," she weakly insisted.

She tried to push away again, but her limbs felt so heavy that she could barely move them. Jenelle was all but powerless as Rourke guided her down the hall to the lone bedroom in the apartment. Once they had reached the bed, he stopped supporting her and gravity took over as she dropped onto the bed. Desperation started to set in as her groggy mind began to piece together what was happening. Her fears were all but confirmed when Rourke slowly closed the bedroom door with that unsettling smile spread across his face.

"You know … when I saw you from across the room all I could think was 'damn, she is a fucking dime piece'," Rourke said as he took his time sauntering over to the bed. "Too bad she probably won't even look my way." He smirked. "Of course, all it took was a little something special in your drink and everything changed. That's all it ever takes with you stuck-up bitches."

Jenelle watched helplessly as Rourke took his sweet time in removing his shorts. She didn't want to keep focusing on him so she glanced to her left as far as she could. At the edge of her vision, standing in the corner of the room, was the well-dressed man who had disappeared earlier. His face remained stoic, and he simply stared at her with a strange persistence lurking in his eyes. The bed moving brought her focus back to the scumbag who had drugged her as he fumbled his way over the mattress toward her. Though his underwear was still on she could see he was hard, and this fact filled her with a mix of disgust and dread.

"This is gonna be fun," he whispered as he bent down and kissed her lips.

As he pulled back, she could see the violet glow around his nose, shining brighter than it had been before. Her focus remained on the glowing body part as she desperately tried to move any of her appendages. Jenelle thought if she could just punch his nose, that might distract him long enough for her to get free, but her body just wasn't responding. For some reason, her gaze drifted back over to the well-dressed creep in the corner. He made eye contact with her and then gave a subtle nod like he was granting her permission to do something. Rourke kissed her once again, this time holding it for far longer as a wave of bile pushed its way into the back of her mouth. He pulled back and a grunt of satisfaction came from his throat.

She tried once more to get her body to move, and to her surprise, her fingers on her left hand twitched. With some hope driving her, Jenelle put all her effort into getting her left arm to move. Suddenly, it reacted to her brain's commands and rocketed forth, connecting with Rourke's nose. Shock covered her assailant's face as the hit caused him to lose his balance and he fell off her. He grabbed his nose with his hand while rocking back and forth from the pain. She watched her attacker as he got too close to the edge of the bed and ended up falling off it.

Rourke grunted in pain as he hit the floor. After a few seconds, he yelled, "You fucking bitch! I'm bleeding because of you, you piece of shit." He scrambled to his feet pure rage filling his eyes, "I'll beat you fucking senseless, you damn whore!"

Jenelle could only watch in terror as Rourke brought his hands away from his nose and balled them into fists. Blood dripped down from the injured appendage, falling onto his shirtless chest as well as the floor. She didn't know why, but as he raised one of his fists back to strike her, she couldn't help but notice the violet glow had disappeared. There was a moment where a surge of terror filled her stomach as he began his attack, but that was interrupted by the door abruptly swinging open. That was enough to get Rourke to stop, and both their attentions were drawn to the doorway to see Roxy standing there with a look of confusion.

Roxy took a quick assessment of the situation, and then with a scowl asked Rourke, "What the fuck is going on here?"

"This fucking bitch hit me!" Rourke quickly replied as he gestured to his bloody nose.

There was a long pause before Roxy got right in his face and screamed, "That fucking bitch is my friend!" She looked at Jenelle as she asked, "Are you okay?"

Jenelle desperately wanted to respond, to scream out that Rourke had almost raped her, but she still couldn't move. That moment she had been able to punch with her arm was gone and now her body was once again motionless. Using just her eyes, she tried to warn Roxy of the shitbag in front of her. Thankfully, her friend knew her well enough and easily spotted the pain and fear in an instant. A swift kick was delivered to Rourke's groin and the man crumbled to his knees.

"Fuck you!" Roxy screamed at the top of her lungs. "Get the fuck out of here right now you fucking rapist! I'm calling the cops on your ass."

Rourke tried to reach for his pants, but Roxy kicked his hand while she continued to scream at him. Quickly, the sexual predator scrambled to his feet and took off while still almost completely naked. Though Jenelle could only watch, it was still satisfying to see that piece of shit get humiliated as he ran by all the partygoers who were now actively screaming vitriol at him, which was definitely deserved. She listened to all the insults for several moments then looked back at the corner of the room to see the well-dressed man still staring at her, though now he wore a large grin across his face. Apparently, she had done something that pleased the stranger. She blinked and the weird man was gone, leaving her in the bedroom alone with her confusion.

FIVE
DIARY ENTRY: JUNE 7TH, 1908

I finally did it. After nine long years, I'm free of that lecherous bastard. Now, all I have to do is play dumb for a while. That will be easy. I've spent my whole life playing dumb. My teachers, my father, that wretch of a husband, I played dumb for them all. My whole life I've been told how stupid I was and how I couldn't make my own choices. A woman making her own choices? How ridiculous of an idea that was to those simple-minded fools. I can play stupid for a little bit longer. I've been doing it for 26 years, what's another one or two on top of that? And once things die down, and those moronic cops aren't snooping around anymore, I'll be free!

I owe it all to that strange man. He showed me how to do it, how to take back my life. Not with his words, but his actions. The simple nod of his head. That slight change between his scowl and his smile. Those small things he did, they guided me. They gave me the strength and the courage to take back what is mine. And now that disgusting pig is gone, dissolved into the ground where he belongs. He's gone. Every single piece of him is no more. That's why they'll never be able to find the body—because there isn't one.

My only regret is that I don't know who that strange man is. I don't know his name or where he comes from. I don't even know what his voice sounds like. For someone who gave me my freedom, I feel guilty that I know nothing of him. I suppose it's for the best. How good can someone be if they spend their free time coaching people how to kill their cheating spouses? I like to pretend he's an angel that was sent to free me from my misery, but deep down I'm well aware that isn't true. There was something strange about him. I could feel that at the very least. He had an unsettling presence that I'd never felt before. It was almost supernatural.

There was a power about him, but he didn't show it. He didn't have to. Maybe ... maybe that's why I can't get him out of my head. He was the first man I've known who didn't have to whip out his dick just to prove how strong he was. The epitome of an iron fist wrapped in a velvet glove all pressed inside of a puzzle that I can't help but be drawn to. I know that he is dangerous despite never actually seeing him do anything violent. My instincts tell me that I should avoid him at all costs. We will see if I follow those instincts. If I never see him again, then so be it. I will live my life and that will be that. But if he does show up again, I will find out who he is. Or at the very least, I will find out what he is after.

SIX

THE LINE THAT MUST BE DRAWN

The dull pain in her joints was starting to take its toll as she moved down the sidewalk. She made a conscious effort to force her legs to move as normally as possible, but the aches were doing their best to hinder that. Everything felt like it was going to catch on fire at any moment. Jenelle could barely think straight through all the various bolts of agony attacking her body. It had been foolish to wait so long to take care of it, but her reluctance was warranted. Less time had passed than usual before the agony had set in, and for a day or so it seemed as though it was simply related to old age. It was all too clear now though; that constant pain was telling her that payment was due.

A familiar sensation fluttered in her gut, and she realized she was close to her target. Anxiously, she continued to trek down the sidewalk while each step sent an unpleasant tingling racing through her feet. She wanted to move faster—her growing anxiety was goading her to do so—but Jenelle's flesh was too far riddled with pain. Instead of picking up her pace into a moderately fast walk, she kept at the same speed that one would have if they were meandering about a gift shop with time to kill.

Unfortunately, the one thing she didn't have on her side was time. However, she could do nothing more but keep moving while the fluttering in her stomach told her how close she was getting.

She pushed herself forward on the sidewalk while narrowly avoiding others. All her focus was spent on simply moving so people had to maneuver to get out of her way. Several times she bumped into someone but there was no attention given to it and she just kept up her slow walk over the concrete. Eventually, Jenelle reached a crosswalk where she paused to identify where the sensation in her gut was telling her to go, then took a left turn. After pushing down another block or so she came across a mother outside a café with her baby. The infant wailed and screeched while the young caregiver desperately tried to calm down her child. That's when the sensation in Jenelle's stomach reached a crescendo, and for a moment, the unbearable pain filling her body subsided.

It was clear that she had reached her goal, now the next step was learning which part she was to take for herself. Without noticeably slowing her pace, Jenelle moved passed the overwhelmed mother, quickly scanning the woman for the undeniable violet glow that should have been there. Instead, she became confused as the colored shine she was expecting was not present anywhere on the young lady. She continued to move past the café as a way to look inconspicuous, but the pain returned after taking only a few steps beyond the mother. Driven by the returning, intense aches as well as confusion, she came to a stop and then turned back to face the woman.

As the young mother performed a light bounce while shooshing her infant, Jenelle studied her as closely as she could without making it obvious. This did nothing but exacerbate her confusion and she decided to glance around the area for the sign of anyone else who had the potential to be a target. A quick scan brought her focus across the street where the familiar blackened outline of a man stood motionless. She felt the sentient shadow staring at her, though it had no eyes or any actual features to speak of. It was a completely blackened figure devoid of any detail, which was a new development for her. The last time she had seen it, there had still been a pair of piercing eyes poking through the darkness, but those were not present anymore. Regardless, its appearance could only mean one thing; she was in the right place, and since there was no one else nearby, the mother was to be the next sacrifice.

Jenelle stared at the shadowed being while taking in a few deep breaths to prepare herself for the coming task. Slowly, she approached the woman and her baby while the guiding sensation in her stomach became mixed with anxiety. She came to a stop just a few feet from the mother and once again scanned her for the violet glow. This drew the attention of the young woman who locked eyes with her.

They held each other's gaze for a moment, and then the mother said over the wailing of her child, "I'm sorry. I've been trying to calm her down, but she just won't. This hasn't ever happened before."

Jenelle looked at the woman's child, the infant's body pressed against her mother while her back faced the world, and a wave of dread crashed over her. Plain as day, there was the shine she had been looking for faintly emitting from the baby's back. She frantically tried to explain away what she was seeing, but there was no getting around it. The mother was not her target. This realization froze her in place and all the drive she had possessed to appease the shadowed being came to a halt. She tried to decide what to do next, but she had been thrown for a loop. There was no denying it, she had been completely taken by surprise. Her mind was stuck without any thought materializing until she finally realized that she had been staring for far too long. She took in a deep breath and opened her mouth, words stalling on the tip of her tongue. A concerned look came over the mother's face, and it seemed as though she was going to back away.

Before that could happen, Jenelle finally spoke. "I bet it's a tummy ache." There was a long pause of silence and then she explained, "It's probably a tummy ache, that's why it's crying."

The young woman wore an incredulous look as she asked, "Why do you say that?"

"It's the crying. There's a distinct sound … I can't really explain it. Just … after being around enough wailing babies, you pick up on the differences in their crying."

"Oh," the mother quietly replied as her baby continued to bawl. "Do you … work for a nursery or something?"

Jenelle shook her head. "No, no, I'm just a mother. I've had two of my own, so I know a little bit about this stuff." She noticed a shift in the young mother's body language, a very subtle movement, but it was clear that she had relaxed a bit. Seeing an opportunity, she asked while holding her arms out, "May I?"

There was the briefest moment of hesitation combined with a look of worry, then the mother gently placed the baby into Jenelle's arms. She was shocked. Her little ploy had worked and now she had her sacrifice in hand. She could feel the presence of the shadowed being growing stronger, its will coating the air around her like a thick smog. It was all too easy. She could take off down the street and the cosmic entity would make sure she got away. Yet, that's not what she did. Instead, she looked at the baby, its face red and scrunched as it cried. Even in a state of discomfort, the infant was adorable, and even more so, it had an aura of innocence around it.

Her hesitation did not go unnoticed as a light wave of pain shot up her spine, reminding her of the task at hand. She was mere moments from spinning around and making a run for it when the thought of her own children flittered through her mind. They were fully grown now, both moved out, but they had once been like the infant she held in her hands. That's when she cycled through the joyous moments she witnessed in her children's lives. Their first steps, all the conversations had, the board games played on rainy days, those precious memories that made her life worth living. Those moments had made all the evil things she had done worth it, but was she willing to do that now? Would not only taking the future away from a baby, but also robbing a young mother of the joys that she herself had experienced, really be worth it for a few more pain-free months or years?

With no more hesitation, she lifted the baby and placed its head on the top of her shoulder. Gently, she applied the same method she had once perfected with her children while turning her gaze to view the shadowed presence that remained motionless in the same place she had initially spotted it. The infant's wails continued for a few more moments until a strong burb was expelled from its mouth. Jenelle felt something wet against the fabric of her shirt, but she didn't care. She could sense the air shift, filling with an aura of dissatisfaction that was directed at her. Just as the child began to calm down, a wave of agony bubbled up through her legs and she had to struggle with all her might to keep steady. She held strong, forcing a small smile as the babe's body finally relaxed.

"Here you go," Jenelle whispered as she gingerly handed the infant back to its mother.

"That was incredible," the young mother quietly exclaimed. "I owe you one."

That small comment made Jenelle smile. Even as the cosmic being ramped up the agony coursing through her, there was still a part of her that managed to feel good thanks to the appreciation of the mother.

"It was nothing," she replied and then winced as a ball of pain ripped into her gut. "I was just glad I could help. You don't owe me a damn thing."

"Well, whatever you did, you gotta …"

Jenelle stopped listening to the young woman's words as a wave of agony ripped through her entire body. Every limb, muscle, joint, and ligament radiated pain that was so intense her mind could not concentrate on anything else. She glanced over to see that the shadowed being had still not moved, and she doubted it would do so any time soon. That meant there was a small window, a tiny hint that she could relieve some of the agony that swept through her, but she had to move quickly. As the young mother continued to talk, Jenelle turned and tried to walk away. A hot burning sensation rocketed through her feet with each step, so she found herself moving along in a hobbled motion.

"Are … are you okay?"

Jenelle was only half listening as she incoherently yelled over her shoulder, "I have a meeting!"

She continued to hobble down the street, gradually putting distance between her and the cosmic being that was tormenting her. It wasn't until she had forced her body to keep moving for a little over a block that she realized the pain wasn't subsiding. If anything, the unbearable sensations assailing her body were getting worse. That's when she realized there was no escaping this. The shadowed being wasn't going to allow her to go against its wishes without facing consequences. After all the terrible things she had done to prolong her life, one good deed would be her undoing. Jenelle had to face the facts. There was no way around it, she was going to die.

SEVEN
DIARY ENTRY: MARCH 13TH, 1915

He visited again last night. I could sense he was there before I even saw him. There's a feeling that I have, this strange sense of connection whenever he shows up. It seems that me and him are connected now, in more ways than one. I know he's not of this world, and I don't care. He liberated me from my husband and I will be forever grateful for that. The police never came back after that first round of initial questions. I guess it makes sense, it wasn't like there was a body for them to find. But more than that, I think he had something to do with it. He wasn't just helping me out, there was something in it for him.

Either way, I have so many questions about him, but I do not care if they are answered. The only thing I need to know is that his power is far beyond that of any mere man. More importantly, he gives me some of that strength. I know he does. I can feel it each time I enact his will. He's never spoken, only gestures at most, but I know exactly what to do. The first time was easy. My husband deserved it, and my rage fueled my actions. But the second one ... the time before this one ... it was harder. I admit to that. She was a stranger. I didn't know anything about her. That disconnect, the fact that she hadn't harmed me in any way, it made things difficult. But the power that I felt after? The rush of energy that coursed through my body and the complete absence of pain? That made it worth it.

That feeling of strength, I held onto it in my mind until he came last night. He appeared out of thin air as he had before, just standing at the foot of my bed. Truth be told, I knew he would be coming soon. My hands, the aches, had been getting worse. It had become unbearable. I could barely use them, but that could be fixed. He showed me with nods and gestures what to do and I followed his silent directions to the bar. It was far enough away, probably forty miles from where I live. That's enough distance for them not to suspect me. I spotted it the moment I entered. That violet glow, wrapped around some man's hands.

Of course, I faced some resistance from everybody in the bar. After all, a woman isn't supposed to be in a place like that. The fucking pigs really think that a woman couldn't drink them under the table, how pathetic. All those angry glances didn't matter the second I started getting cozy with my target. He gave in so easily after a little flirting, and from there his fate was sealed. I proceeded to fill him with liquor until he could barely speak, then led him out into the night. Then, my mysterious man gave me the signal, and I disposed of the drunk with a few stabs. The man was so intoxicated that the first few cuts with my knife didn't even register. After that, I took his hands, and my partner took the rest.

It was all too easy, and I have no doubt that my friend will make sure no one even thinks of tying me to that man's disappearance. My pain is completely gone and once again I can feel this otherworldly energy flowing through me. There is so much I can get done. So many things I can do with this strength. I wonder how long this new power will remain. My only hope is that it stays for a few weeks, then I'll patiently await his return.

EIGHT
A NICE HELPING OF BELATED
JUSTICE

She caught sight of him while pretending to stare at the menu. There was a dumb, confused look plastered across his face that she immediately despised. She watched him scan the restaurant, passing over her several times, somehow not able to spot her. Finally, she waved to him and managed to get his attention. He flashed a wide grin and then made his way over to the table, nearly bumping into a waiter in the process. As he took a seat, she noticed he was wearing the same type of clothing he had been at the party the night he tried to force himself on her. An unbridled rage bubbled in her gut as she thought about that night, but she managed to keep it to herself. Soon enough, she would have retribution, she just had to be patient for a little longer.

"Um ... Jenelle, right?" Rourke asked as he loudly scooted his chair closer to the table.

Jenelle gave a small nod while forcing a smile. "Yup ... and ... Rourke?"

"Yeah, you got it," Rourke chuckled. "Sorry, I had to think for a minute for your name. That kegger was wild and I was pretty blasted when we bumped into each other. But I guess you were in the same boat too, huh?"

Jenelle just stared with a small smile while seething with rage. Of course, she remembered his name. She had kept it with her for eleven months since that night, letting it fester in her mind like an open wound. Then a few weeks ago, the man with the outdated clothes appeared to her. He had just been standing in the middle of her dorm, wearing the same emotionless expression from the party. She had read her great-great-grandmother's diary over and over, preparing for that moment, so once he was standing there, she was ready. That was when she realized she hadn't finished what she started with Rourke. He didn't just owe a little blood from a busted nose, much more of him would be required to pay his debt.

So, she had covertly started asking around about him. She began with her friends who had been there that night, then branched out to acquaintances and finally tapped into the fraternity crowd. That's when she learned which fraternity Rourke belonged to and her plan began to form. Everything she had done since then had been calculated. Sneaking into that kegger. "Bumping" into Rourke when he was three sheets to the wind and making damn sure to leave an impression. Of course, the piece of resistance was leaving her number, so he called her. That made it so much easier to convince him that the date was his idea and that he was the one making the decisions. It was a great way to keep his simple mind distracted and not asking too many questions.

"Are you a diner type of gal or something?" Rourke inquired as he glanced around the somewhat rundown place.

She tried to keep from rolling her eyes as she replied, "It's cheap, which is nice since I'm a poor college student."

He nodded. "That makes sense. Morton U can be expensive, they're certainly bending me over now that I don't have a baseball scholarship anymore."

Jenelle didn't try to correct him by saying she was actually attending Hallowhall, because she had already told him that almost a year ago. It was a nice confirmation that he truly didn't remember a damn thing about her. She had just been a prize he was after, nothing more. Normally, that would infuriate her, but his entitlement and ignorance were beneficial to her right now. Plus, the details about herself didn't matter, the only thing that did was making the date a fun and easy experience for Rourke. Lull him into a feeling of comfort so she could carry out the final part of her plan.

"Well, I'm starving, so I hope you don't mind me getting some apps," Rourke said as he glanced over the menu with a clear eager look spread across his face.

Jenelle smiled, a genuine one this time as she realized how easy it was going to be to keep this dimwitted asshole content. "Not at all. The mozz sticks are a good choice, but their salsa is supposed to be good too."

That was all she really needed to say. From that point on she let him have full reign of the conversation and he took advantage. He rambled on and on about all his stupid hobbies and the ridiculous side hustles he had been doing with his friends. Every sentence that left his mouth screamed to Jenelle that he was a douche, which helped reaffirm that what she was going to do was the right thing. Surprisingly, her opening came rather early on, just a minute or two after the chips and salsa arrived. When Rourke obnoxiously excused himself to take a leak, she pulled out the little concoction she had whipped up a few nights prior and dumped it into the salsa. A little stirring was all it took, and the powder dissolved into the dip without a trace.

Her only anxious moment during the dinner was when Rourke came back from the restroom and didn't touch the salsa right away. She couldn't help but keep glancing at the dip out of the corner of her eye, while her muscles were tensed up. Finally, after finishing his explanation of the subtle differences in batting styles in baseball, he scooped up a decent bit of salsa and shoveled the chip into his mouth. Jenelle didn't fully relax until he had done it a few more times, but she was confident he had ingested more than enough for the desired effect. Sure enough, by the end of the meal, Rourke seemed to be a little lethargic. He definitely had slowed down a bit and she noticed his eyes were a little duller thanks to what was circulating through his bloodstream. She needed to get him out of there before he passed out in the middle of the diner.

With a rather rude snap of her fingers, she called over the waiter and paid for their meal (Rourke didn't object to it) with almost all the money in her wallet. She would be broke for a few weeks, but it was more than worth it. Then, she stood up and escorted her date out of the diner. By this point, he was beginning to stumble a bit and had started to slur his words. Despite his mumbling to be taken to his car, she directed him over to hers. By the time she had him buckled in the passenger seat and was pulling out of the parking lot, he was already unconscious. From there she drove fifteen minutes to a park on the outskirts of town. It was a secluded enough place for her task, with minimal traffic around the area, but enough lighting for her to see what she was doing.

Once parked, she lowered the passenger seat so Rourke wasn't so scrunched up, and began to search for the same kind of shine she saw at the party almost a year ago. It didn't take long until she spotted a violet glow coming from the left side of his body around where his stomach was. Jenelle reached back for her tools but let out a yelp of surprise upon noticing the man in outdated clothes sitting silently in her backseat. She hesitated, but then he gave a simple nod, and she snatched up the drawstring bag she had brought. From there she rummaged around before producing a kitchen knife.

There was no hesitation, no moment of weakness before she plunged the blade into Rourke's side. All the pent-up rage that had been festering for quite some time was finally released by a spurt of blood pouring from her aggressor. A sudden scream came from Rourke's mouth and he opened his eyes. In a panic, Jenelle withdrew the knife and stabbed him again, this time hitting the middle of his gut. He cried out in agony with shock etched across his face, clearly too confused to mount any kind of counterattack. She withdrew the blade once more and then repeatedly brought it down, making shallow punctures all over his torso. He struggled for a few more moments, but the blood was spilling out far too quickly and his life along with it.

Jenelle took a few seconds to calm down, then turned to the silent gentleman behind her. "What now?" she asked.

He wordlessly gestured to Rourke in response but that didn't clarify much for her. She scanned the deceased's body and noticed that the small area on his left side was still aglow in a soft, violet hue.

"Am I … supposed to cut something out of him?" she hesitantly inquired.

A simple nod told her all she needed to know. Jenelle studied the part of the body, deciding how best to go about ripping it open. She searched through her drawstring bag and took out several other knives she had brought. There was hesitation before the first cut. Now that the gore was in front of her and she had to stare at it, she felt a bit squeamish. Regardless, she set to work, cutting away chunks of flesh while keeping a close eye on that soft shine. Her hands quickly became covered in blood and the slickness made it difficult to grip the various knives, but she continued. Finally, she located the organ that had been shining with the violet glow, a small reddish-brown body part that she assumed was a kidney. She hacked away the last bit of flesh to free it, then pulled the organ out of the corpse.

She looked back to the silent man and asked, "What am I supposed to do with this?"

He silently pointed at the organ that Jenelle was holding, then to her, and finally gestured to his mouth.

"You … you want me to eat it?" she said in disbelief. "Yeah, that ain't happening."

Suddenly, a torrent of pain exploded on her left side, crippling her body. The agony was so great that her throat froze up and she couldn't even scream in response to it. In a moment, it was all over and she was given a chance to catch her breath. She gently prodded her side while still holding the dripping organ in her other hand. No pain came from her touch, so she allowed herself a sigh of relief.

"Okay, I get it," she said with a grimace.

Jenelle stared at the kidney, studying the body part in the small bits of lamplight that crept into her car. With a great deal of reluctance, she lifted it to her mouth and tried to take a bite, but the metallic taste made her gag. She pulled it back from her lips while heaving a little bit.

"I … I can't do it," she insisted.

The man shook his head in disappointment, then closed his eyes for a moment. Gingerly, he touched Jenelle's shoulder then pulled back his hand. With a small nod, he commanded her to try once more. She shuddered, wanting nothing more than to throw the kidney away, but she knew that would be a very bad move. The stranger in outdated clothing was something far more than just an ordinary person, and it would be beyond stupid to cross him. So, with a trembling hand, she brought the kidney back up to her mouth and slowly bit into it. To her surprise, she was met by a completely different taste than before. This time, there was no distinct flavor of blood, but something sweet instead. It almost reminded her of the store-bought cookies with the colored frosting on top. The new flavor made it much easier to take another bite and then another. In a matter of minutes, she had snarfed down half of the kidney before feeling her stomach groan in protest.

"I'm done," she declared in between gasps for air. "I can't eat anymore."

The silent man looked at her with an icy gaze that filled her with dread, but then he simply nodded in approval. Wordlessly, he reached over and placed a hand on top of Rourke's head. A few seconds of stillness passed, and then the corpse began to shake. Suddenly, the flesh condensed, falling in on itself. From there it was sucked into the stranger's hand, disappearing into his body. Jenelle made eye contact with the man who flashed a toothy grin at her, then vanished, leaving her alone. Without a body. Without any blood or viscera staining the upholstery. She was left alone by herself to contemplate what the hell had just happened.

NINE

IT'S JUST A GRADUATION

The arena was roughly half full with families interspersed throughout. Normally the place would be filled with a cheering crowd and a ruckus student section, but there was no game being played today. It was graduation instead, and it was clear just based on the numbers in attendance that this wasn't one of the college's stronger crops of students. Except for Simon of course, Jenelle's firstborn and an impressive Summa Cum Laude graduate with a degree in engineering. She was so proud of him and everything he had accomplished. Of course, it would have been much easier to take pride in his success if her right leg wasn't ripped with constant pain. The agony had been tormenting her for over a week now, but she hoped she could hold out a few more days.

"Shit, we've probably got another hour of sitting here," Jonathan whispered in her ear. "I swear, graduations are the only time I'm not happy with my last name."

Jenelle wanted to get after him for complaining, but an eruption of agony caused her body to seize up. She instinctively grabbed hold of the afflicted limb and did her best to stifle a cry that was desperately trying to escape her lungs. The situation was becoming too much for her to handle; she was going to have to act before the day was through. That's when she saw it standing in the aisle made of concrete steps, just a few rows of bleachers from her. The entity was almost completely comprised of ethereal shadow except for a pair of piercing eyes that she knew all too well. They were the same eyes that had guided her to perform unspeakable acts over the years, and they were back once more. This was different from the other times though. The being had never shown itself at such an inopportune time before. It was clear that it was there to force her hand.

She got to her feet and stumbled a bit as another wave of pain shot through her affected limb. Jenelle was barely able to keep herself from falling by grabbing hold of the seat in front of her, causing the person sitting there to shoot her a glare.

"Are you okay, hon?" Jonathan asked as he lightly placed a hand on the back of her waist.

"I'm fine," she snapped while smacking his hand away. Regret immediately filled her chest and she said in a much calmer tone, "I just need to use the bathroom. My stomach is killing me. It's nothing though, I'll be fine."

Quickly, she shuffled her way to the end of the row and out onto the concrete steps, all while the cosmic being stared at her. She could feel its gaze as she climbed the steps, which certainly wasn't helping her keep her footing. Jenelle had to grip the metal railing for support, squeezing it with all her might with each new tremor of agony coursing up her leg. Finally, she reached the top of the steps and hurried toward the bathroom. As she limped about, the shadowed being would appear a few dozen feet in front of her, constantly reminding her it was there. A cold sweat broke out on her forehead and nausea crept up alongside every other horrible sensation she was experiencing.

The door to the women's restroom was heavier than she anticipated, so it hurt a bit when she slammed into it and it didn't easily open for her. A forceful push with both arms sent the door flying open and slamming against the stopper that kept it from scuffing the concrete wall. Jenelle hobbled into the lavatories, barely managing to reach the sinks before her afflicted leg gave out on her. The counter stopped her from totally falling, but her right elbow slammed down against the sturdy material. A new ripple of pain moved through her body, connecting with the one emanating from her leg and making an unbearable situation even worse.

"Are … you okay?" a timid voice asked.

Jenelle whipped her head in the direction of the question and spotted a younger-looking woman, probably mid-twenties. It took her mind a few moments to truly process the words, and then a couple of seconds more to respond with labored breath, "Yeah, I just …" She stopped abruptly as she noticed the young lady's left leg, bathed in a subtle violet glow. "… I tripped," she finally managed to spit out.

The woman tentatively approached a sink roughly fifteen feet or so away from where Jenelle was. "Okay, I wanted to be sure you weren't hurt or anything like that," the lady spoke, clearly uncomfortable with the situation.

Jenelle didn't reply, her focus fixated on the shine coming from the flustered woman. She mulled over what to do in her mind as the only other person in the bathroom washed her hands. Would it be worth the risk to go for it and such a public place? A surge of agony pumped itself through her leg as if telling her what her choice should be. She let out an audible gasp as her fingers gripped the countertop tighter. The young woman was staring out of the corner of her eye and pretending to continue to wash her hands while trying to decide what to do next. There was a palpable tension in the air as both women waited for the other to do something. Finally, Jenelle made the first move by pulling herself up to where she was fully standing. She then ever so slowly limped toward the nearest open stall. As she went to close the stall door, the two made eye contact, their gazes hanging there for an extended moment before the divider broke the connection.

She pressed her hand against the left wall of the stall for support as she reached into the small, hidden pocket on her dress. As gently as possible, Jenelle removed the pocketknife she had expertly hidden on her person and flipped it open. The sound of running water ceased and she frantically glanced through the small crack of the stall to try to get a glimpse of what was happening. A loud sigh reached her ears, and she realized the young woman was still in the room. She assumed that the young lady's next move would be leaving the bathroom as quickly and quietly as possible, which meant she would have to make her move first.

The muscles in her arms tensed as she prepared for the risky move she was about to make. She hadn't latched the stall closed so a simple push would throw it wide open. Her nerves got the better of her limbs and she ended up using a little too much force, flinging the stall door and causing it to slam against the one right next to it. The young woman had already started to head for the exit, but the sudden commotion took her by surprise. As Jenelle raced forth with the knife gripped tightly in her right hand, the young lady spun around to look at her with a face filled with confusion and fear. The woman managed to register what was happening a mere second before the knife stabbed through the air, connecting with the right side of her torso, just below the ribcage.

"F-f-fuck you! Fuck you!" the injured woman screamed as blood leaked from the wound.

She threw a punch that lightly connected with Jenelle's left arm, but that certainly wasn't enough to do anything. A small tug was all it took to pull the knife free. Based on the amount of blood coming from the damaged area, the cut wasn't very deep.

"Get the fuck back!" the young lady screamed.

Jenelle gave a quick stab, this one landing a few inches

further up on her victim's torso. Cries of pain filled the bathroom, bouncing off the linoleum-covered walls. After the third strike, she found a rhythm, her attacks coming one after the other in quick succession. The thrusts weren't precise in any way, but they found flesh, and that was what mattered. Suddenly, the woman grabbed hold of her right arm, stopping another thrust from happening.

"P-Please d-don't kill me," the woman pleaded as blood poured from the corners of her mouth.

Right then, an overwhelming feeling of guilt welled up inside of Jenelle. She looked her victim in the eyes as she whispered, "I'm sorry … but I have to do this."

She stabbed into the woman's gut with as much force as she could muster, hoping that would end things. A few twists of the knife while the blade was embedded inside flesh, then she withdrew it. The life had all but faded from the dying woman, but there was just enough for a gagging sound to emanate from the victim's throat. Slowly, Jenelle released her hold on the lady and watched as her body fell to the floor. She stood there, shaking as she still held the knife firmly in her blood-soaked hand. Remorse filled her as she stared down at the fresh corpse riddled with stab wounds. If she hadn't come along, this person probably could have gone on to great things. They were certainly young enough that they would have had a lot of life in front of them, and she snuffed all that out.

A sudden sting of pain pulled her focus away from her guilt and directed it back to why she had mercilessly torn someone apart in a bathroom. The violet glow still surrounded the woman's leg, waiting for Jenelle to take what was hers. She dropped down to her knees and pulled the body closer to her to the point where the radiating leg was only inches from her lips. There was hesitation thanks to the memories of how raw flesh tasted, but another assailment of agony quickly put a stop to that. She bit into the calf as hard as possible, then tugged with her teeth, fighting with ferocity to rip a small chunk free.

The taste overwhelmed her and she gagged for a moment, but forced herself to keep from spitting the flesh out. She chewed quickly, and only what was needed to tenderize the meat enough for her to swallow. Once her mouth was empty a familiar sensation washed over her. The feeling of power coursed through her veins and all hesitation was tossed to the side. She eagerly ripped into the thigh, tearing off chunks of flesh at an alarming rate. Her focus remained solely on devouring as much of the limb as possible until the sound of echoing footsteps reached her ears. Someone was headed toward the restroom. She had to move, and fast.

Jenelle climbed to her feet while still holding onto the gnawed-on leg. She readjusted her grip and then pulled on the corpse, dragging it across the bathroom floor. The strength from her snack powered every fiber of her muscles and the body was easy to move to the nearest stall. She pulled the corpse inside then reached forward and slammed the stall door shut just as the sound of footsteps entered the bathroom. Several tense moments went by where there were no other noises besides footsteps and her breathing, and then the sounds of footfall stopped. Out of impulse, she sucked in her breath and held it, bathing the room in silence.

The quiet was shattered by a terror-filled scream as someone shouted, "Oh my god! There's blood everywhere!"

"Fuck, we have to get someone," another person shouted.

"Fuck this! Fuck this!" the first voice replied.

The screams quickly moved out and away from the restroom, leaving Jenelle alone with the body. There was no way whoever it was could have seen her, so for the moment her identity remained safe. However, they would be coming back soon, with security in tow. Finally, panic set in and she acted quickly by tearing into the leg once again. She frantically ripped as much meat from the bone as she could hoping to reach the unspecified quota of cannibalism. Bite after bite she chowed down while desperately hoping the shadowed entity would arrive. Suddenly, the outline of the shadowed being phased through the wall of the stall, stopping only a few inches from her face.

"Oh shit!" Jenelle yelped in surprise as a chunk of flesh fell from her mouth. "Fuck me!" she exclaimed while tossing down the body.

The eyes of the cosmic entity glanced at her for only a moment, then redirected their attention to the corpse. A completely black hand stretched forth and began to absorb what was left of the body into its essence. In a matter of seconds, everything had been sucked up and the being disappeared a moment later. Jenelle was left in the stall by herself with a heart that was beating against her chest. She stumbled out and over to the sinks where she slammed her hands down on the countertop. With heavy breathing she glanced up at her reflection, relieved to find it lacking a single trace of blood. Despite how clean her face looked, she turned on the faucet and grabbed a cupped handful of water, splashing it on her visage. She then hastily exited the restroom, drying her face by using the sleeve of her shirt. As she walked, three women and two security guards came into view, running in her direction. Her anxiety skyrocketed upon seeing them, but she choked down the natural urge to run and tried to look as inconspicuous as possible.

"Hey, you!" one of the guards called out as they approached her. The group slowed to a stop as they caught up to her and the guard asked, "Did you just come from the bathrooms?"

Jenelle's heart beat so fast it felt like it was going to rip itself right out of her chest. She locked eyes with the security man, her fear of getting caught building at a rapid rate. After a deep breath, she replied in a nonchalant tone, "Uh ... no. I was just walking around out here. My legs fell asleep." She forced a fake chuckle then added, "I always forget how long graduations can be."

The guard didn't even ask a follow-up question or respond with a comment. Instead, he and the other four hustled away from her in the direction she had just come from. She waited for a minute or so then let out a sigh. It seemed like she was going to get away with it. After all, there was nothing there for them to find. Only the typical nastiness one expected in a public bathroom would be awaiting them. Meanwhile, Jenelle would return to her seat and sit through the remainder of the commencement. Hopefully, it would be over soon so she didn't have to sit there with her thoughts. The last thing she wanted to do was replay what she had just done in her mind. Especially because her thoughts would eventually turn to the taste, and how after the first bite she had somewhat enjoyed it.

TEN
DIARY ENTRY: SEPTEMBER 18TH, 1928

Over the past two decades, I've learned one simple fact—all men are stupid. An attractive woman is all it takes for them to lower their guard. It works every single time. In fact, it's becoming far too easy. There is no challenge in killing these simple-minded buffoons. A little flirting followed by a few well-placed stabs and I can enjoy my feast, and more importantly, the energy that comes with it. The thrill has left the whole ordeal. I would not say that the task itself has become mundane, but it most certainly has lost some of its luster.

Maybe that's why I tried my hand at slaying more than one person at a time last night. In hindsight, it was a foolish move, but in the moment there was such a rush that I had never experienced before. Even as I write and recollect on it, I can feel my adrenaline begin to rise. What a glorious feeling! It's a shame I will probably never experience it again. It's far too dangerous to attempt something like it again, for more than one reason. But I will continue to cling to the memory of that brief and intense skirmish.

There was something so satisfying about the whole ordeal that I can't put into words. It had gone like most of the other *times I have done it. I found the man, his chest aglow in that familiar hue of color that I've come to recognize so easily. My seduction seemed to go off without a hitch, with it taking mere moments for him to be eating out of the palm of my hand. It wasn't until he had bought me a second drink that I realized the two gentlemen watching intently from across the room. They were not subtle about it. Amateurs no doubt. Clearly, they lacked the experience needed to make me worry, but the numbers were in their favor. Three against one would certainly leave me at a disadvantage, yet I didn't retreat. Of course, part of my staying put was because my powerful friend would just make me return for the doomed man sooner rather than later. But part of me wanted to experience a true challenge once again.*

So I stuck around, had a few more drinks, and let the morons think they were in control. When my violet-glowing target led me outside, he had this cocky grin spread across his face that I was all too eager to wipe away. The situation fell perfectly into my lap when I was led down a long alleyway and the two cohorts of my liaison showed themselves. I can still vividly remember the looks of confidence on all three of their faces. Even more so, I keep recalling the expression of absolute shock that came over them when I delivered a stab to the gut of my escort.

He was soft. That one stab dispatched him to the ground, and he was no longer a problem. His two friends on the other hand, were far more of a challenge. They managed to land a few blows on me before I was able to return the favor with my knife. The pain of their punches and kicks was ... exquisite. More than anything it made me feel alive. Excited me even. With that kind of motivation, they didn't stand a chance. I wore them down by allowing them to pummel my body, while my will remained completely unharmed.

My opening came after they had beaten me to the ground. They were not expecting me to grab hold of one of their feet, and they certainly weren't expecting a knife to be dragged across their Achilles tendon. What an incredibly effective and satisfying way to incapacitate such filth. Of course, this efficiency took the last man standing by surprise, which gave me another opening to drive my knife into his left upper thigh. That being said, while I had been busy dispatching his friends, my true target had crawled his way back toward the opening of the alley. Even in my badly beaten state, it was easy to catch up to him. A well-executed throat slice was all I needed to gain control of the situation.

My powerful benefactor appeared just as I had taken care of the first man. Over the past few years, more and more of him has become permanently cloaked in complete darkness, but not those piercing eyes of his. It was difficult to spot him against the darkness of the night, but those eyes alerted me to his presence. In an instant, I could tell he wanted me to rip out the glowing part of the man before me and get it over with, but there were two more people I had to contend with. In what came as a surprise to me, he followed close behind as I went back to the two men who were crying for help.

I decided to take my time with both men to repay them for what they had done to my body. Sure, I would heal after my feast, but they still had to be punished for what they did. The blade easily sliced through flesh, and I made sure to create shallow cuts all over their bodies after I had taken their limbs out of commission. Halfway through my carving spree, I realized that the pain and suffering I was inflicting brought me pleasure. Each cut filled me with a rush of ecstasy that nearly matched the sensation I encountered when feasting on the flesh of the selected few.

Eventually, my benefactor grew tired of my pleasure and put a stop to it with a thunderous boom that echoed from his hands being clapped together. He made himself clear. I was to finish my mission immediately, or I would experience how monstrous his strength could be. I had no choice but to obey. After all this time, with everything I've done, I'm still at the whim of a man. My meal was fine. I received my rush of power from tearing apart most of a rather fatty liver, but it wasn't the same as before. I didn't feel as much in control, and that lack of independence has left a bitter taste in my mouth. Now I know what I am truly after, power. The strength to make sure no man ever has any control over me is what I desire more than anything else.

It disgusts me that I might never reach such a goal. After all, if my silent benefactor wasn't there to clean up all the bodies I had left lying in the alley, I would have been fucked for sure. As much as I hate to admit it, I need him. At least for now. Even more annoying, he made it all too clear with a single icy glare that I was not to kill anyone else except those he has designated for me with his violet glow. I am at his mercy since he is the one who grants me this wonderful power. So, I will conform to him for now. Do his bidding until I've gained enough strength of my own to challenge him.

My only fear is that I have limited time to do so. Even though I am imbued with a life force stronger than any normal person, I can feel age begin to creep up on me. It is subtle for now, but I have noticed its work at play. The tiniest aches have made themselves known to my joints, and there is a defining wrinkle now on my right cheek. I still appear far younger than other women my age, but how long will that last? If I do not gain enough strength soon, I fear I will be kept at this powerful being's mercy for the rest of my life. That is something I cannot allow to happen.

ELEVEN

A BREAK FROM STUDYING

The library was empty, though that was to be expected. Even though the building was open twenty-four hours a day, most students didn't even bother trying to go there if it was past ten. Jenelle was the exception. Nights were the best time to get most of her research and studying done as well as having plenty of opportunity to be left alone with her thoughts. Ever since she had taken care of Rourke, she had been spending quite a lot of time in silent contemplation. Large chunks of her day were passed replaying that event in her mind even though it had taken place well over a year ago. It was such a surreal thing to know that she had not only killed a man, but eaten part of him too.

Part of the reason she continued to remain hung up on what she had done had to do with the brutality of it. The blood, the viscera, those were things she probably would never forget. The other reason though, was she wondered if she would ever do it again. When she had gone through with it and actually executed her plan, Jenelle had told herself that it was nothing more than revenge. She was adamant that she could never do anything like that again, but what if she was wrong? Her great-great-grandmother certainly liked to kill people, that was all too clear from reading her diary. What if killing was a genetic trait and by taking revenge on Rourke, she had kickstarted her own journey down the horrific path?

Regardless, all the self-contemplation and what-ifs wouldn't matter if that strangely dressed man showed back up. Based on what she had read from her great-great-grandmother's diary she would have no choice but to submit to his will. She would be forced to kill again and there would be no weaseling out of it because refusal meant certain death. Thankfully, he hadn't appeared since that night, but Jenelle was always weary. It made life incredibly difficult since she was constantly checking her surroundings.

Any pain she experienced, whether it be a simple headache or the flu, she feared it being a sign that he would soon come to her once more. Recently, there had been an ache that came in her lower back. She had hoped it would just go away, but it continued to linger and managed to get a little worse over the past week or so. Fearful that it was an omen, she had decided to ignore it and push through the pain, but that was becoming unsustainable. Perhaps, it was really nothing more than a common backache from a pulled muscle or something of the like. Maybe she would make an appointment to get the problem looked at by a doctor, but not now. She had a big test coming up in a week or so, and thanks to her mind being constantly preoccupied, she was forced to study twice as hard. There was no reason to focus on anything else except her schoolwork since all those concerns would be waiting for her regardless of what she did.

Jenelle scanned the bookshelf in front of her and found the book she was looking for. She pulled it out from its position amongst the others, causing a light layer of dust to fall toward the floor. It was evident that people didn't frequent this section of the library often and that made it feel like it was fairly isolated. With its tall bookshelves, to her, it seemed like a great place for someone to hide. That in itself was a comforting thought to her. She smiled at the idea of being able to curl up in this place and hide from all the problems or intrusive thoughts that continuously plagued her. That pleasant moment was interrupted by a spasm snaking up her back. The sudden and unpleasant sensation caused her grip to slip on the book and it tumbled from her grasp. Due to the nearly complete silence of the library, the book landing on the carpeted floor seemed to sound like a bomb going off even though it made nothing more than a muffled thud.

"Hello?" a voice called out in a surprised tone. "Is someone there?"

Jenelle didn't respond and instead bent down to pick up the book. When she stood back up, she was startled by a man coming into view. The two made eye contact as the man came to a stop. Silence once again returned to the library as they stared for a few seconds until the guy let out a very faint chuckle.

"Huh," he said, "I thought I was the only one in here. You uh … you startled me there."

Her first instinct was to ignore the guy and write him off as nothing more than a nosy weirdo, but she decided to take a more diplomatic approach to her response. "Sorry, dropped my book," she said as she tucked her reading material under her arm.

He nodded, "I guess I'm not the only one who's burning the midnight oil to study."

"Yup, I guess so," Jenelle replied with a twinge of annoyance. Even if someone was doing a terrible job of it, she could tell when someone was trying to flirt with her and she was not in the mood.

As she turned and started to exit the aisle the man asked, "Mind if I walk with you?"

She did, but she didn't humor him with a response. So, as Jenelle made her way to the front where the tables were located, she had a grown man following close behind with a couple of books of his own in hand.

"Let me guess … Econ 342?" the guy randomly asked.

"What?" Jenelle responded as a knee-jerk reaction.

"You're studying for Econ 342, right?" he replied. When the man was met by silence he hastily added, "I just noticed the book you have. You know, the title of it is a dead giveaway. I hope I didn't creep you out or anything. I wasn't trying to be creepy, really. I'm sorry. My apologies."

The two made it to the area with the tables and Jenelle turned to face the weird guy who had been following her. She stared at him while he looked down at the ground, nervously blushing.

"Again, I'm sorry if I creeped you out."

"Why do you keep saying that?" she inquired, trying to figure out what he was after.

He scratched the back of his head, a nervous tick no doubt. "Well … your reaction to me says it all. I mean, I-I don't blame you, you know? You think you're alone and then some guy comes out of nowhere and starts asking random questions. I understand why that would be off-putting."

Her impatience got the better of her and Jenelle bluntly asked, "Okay, what do you want?"

"What do I …" the man trailed off, confused.

"Yeah, what do you want? Why are you talking to me?"

The clearly flustered man took a few seconds before he finally began replying, "Well … I just … I do a lot …uh … study a lot, at night. You know? There's really no one ever here, and I just thought … thought we could talk."

Based on his body language and how pathetic he sounded Jenelle realized this guy wasn't a threat like Rourke had been. He was nothing more than a lonely nerd looking for a little companionship. She softened a bit to the weirdo standing before her and sat the book in her hand down on the table next to her.

"So, I take it you're in here a lot, huh?" she inquired with a softer tone.

The timid man perked up at hearing her words, lifting his head a bit. "Yeah, yeah I'm in here almost every night."

She glanced at the pile of books he was holding on to and noticed that they covered a variety of different subjects. That made it fairly easy to infer that he chose to be in the library as opposed to having to be there due to some class he was taking. Just to confirm her assumption, she asked, "How long have you been coming here … for fun?"

A look of shock came over the nerd's face in response to Jenelle learning his secret. "H-how?" he stuttered in complete perplexion. When she gestured at the books he was holding he glanced down and the dots connected for him. "Ah … I suppose these are a dead giveaway," he said sitting down his reading collection. "I've been doing it since I came to this university, but really I've been choosing books over people most of my life."

"I can understand that," Jenelle commented, her thoughts flashing with images of ripping Rourke's kidney free from his flesh. "People can be cruel."

"Exactly!" the nerd responded with excitement. There was clear energy in his voice as he said, "Books don't call you names or treat you poorly. And the only ones who tend to stay within the walls of a library are those who appreciate books for what they are. Those are people you can trust."

Jenelle chuckled, "Okay, you've sold me."

Realizing how loud he had gotten, the awkward man shrank a little bit as he said, "Oh, I'm sorry. I didn't mean to be so loud."

His apologies were somewhat endearing to Jenelle. She could tell he was sincere in them, and the more he spoke, the more she felt at ease around him. He was the complete opposite of Rourke. There was no bravado behind his words, nor was there any hint of overconfidence in his demeanor. This was a man who chose learning over the prospect of getting laid, not because he was in search of some academic glory, but because it was his passion. He was safe, and that was comforting to Jenelle. She had barely spoken to a man since her terrible experience, let alone felt safe around one. It was nice to finally be in the company of someone of the opposite sex that she could honestly talk to without feeling uncomfortable.

"Oh, my apologies for not introducing myself, that's rude of me," the nerd said while holding out a hand for Jenelle to shake. They stood in awkward silence until she finally extended her hand, and then the awkward man continued, "My name is Marvin."

"I'm Jenelle," she said in response, not only to be polite but also because she genuinely wanted to get to know Marvin. "So, are you an econ major?" When he gave her a puzzled look she elaborated, "You know, since you were able to tell what course I was in based on my book, I assumed you were an econ major."

"Oh!" Marvin exclaimed with realization. He then shook his head while chuckling, "No, no, I just took the same class. I actually went for accounting."

"Went?" Jenelle repeated, picking up on him using the past tense.

"Well, I already got my undergrad," Marving explained. He seemed flustered once again as he added, "I uh … I'm going for my doctorate in accounting, but I've already got my undergrad in accounting. Hence why I used 'went' … as in the past tense."

Jenelle couldn't help but laugh at his continuing effort to not offend or creep her out in any way possible. He was trying so hard, and she couldn't help but admire it. "Don't worry, I understand what you meant."

"Oh," Marvin responded and then sighed with relief. "Good, good, I didn't want to come off as creepy again."

"Don't worry, Marvin. I've met some real creeps in my life, and you're definitely not one of them."

Marvin visibly blushed. "Oh, well thank you for the compliment. I appreciate it." He paused, then asked, "So, how goes the studying for your test?"

"Not as well as it should, if I'm being honest," she answered with a shrug.

"Oh, is it the material giving you trouble? Because if so, I can help you study," Marvin offered.

She shook her head, "No, it's not that. I just can't focus long enough to actually keep anything in my head. I guess I'm just not in …"

A sudden and searing pain coursing through her lower back cut her off. She instinctively grabbed at the problem area as a clear look of agony spread over her face.

"What? What is it?" Marvin inquired with concern.

Jenelle tried to downplay her suffering as she unconvincingly replied, "It's just a backache. Nothing serious, it took me by surprise is all."

"Are you sure? I think I have some pain medicine in my backpack if you want."

Jenelle shook her head, "It really is nothing." Another wave of agony and her face told a different story.

"I'm just going to check real fast," Marvin said as he turned around to search through his backpack which he had placed on the same table as his stack of books. "You don't have to take it, but it would make me feel better knowing I at least gave you the option."

Jenelle was about to insist that he didn't have to do that, but something caught her eye first that caused her to freeze up. A terrible ball of anxiety twisted her stomach together in knots as she stared at the faint, violet glow that was emanating from Marvin's back. She immediately scanned the area and spotted him standing off to her right, halfway concealed by a bookshelf. No emotion was present on the well-dressed man's face as he nodded, wordlessly giving her the signal to complete her task. A sickening feeling tugged at her gut as she picked up the rather heavy, hardcover book she had sat down earlier and raised it over her head. She closed her eyes, then swung the object as hard as she could. It made contact with a loud smack, followed by a muffled thud.

"W-What … w-why?" said a hurt voice.

Jenelle opened her eyes to spot Marvin lying on the ground in a position where he was able to look up at her. There was fear and confusion on his face, but other than gripping the back of his head, there didn't seem to be any real damage.

"I … I don't understand," he said in shock.

She threw the heavy book and it connected with his face, the impact knocking him back and causing his head to smack against the floor. The blow was enough to stun him and Jenelle grabbed one of the books he had sat down earlier and began to wail on his head. He tried to fend off her attacks, but it was clear he had never been a fighter. After a few smacks with the book, his arms folded from the force of the blows and she had direct access to his head. She continued to assail him, each blow that landed causing a spasm to come from Mavin's body. Gradually, he responded less to the hits and his body's movement decreased. A sickening crack finally sounded and she stopped.

Jenelle set the book down and silently stared at the fractured face oozing blood before her. In between her labored breaths, she glanced up to see the well-dressed man now close enough to leer down at her. "Are you fucking happy now?" she snarled.

The man responded by shaking his head while maintaining an emotionless expression. He then pointed down at the lifeless body while locking eyes with Jenelle. She knew what to do next.

TWELVE
BEFORE GETTING GROCERIES

Jenelle couldn't help but grunt with exertion as she dragged her prize over the uneven ground of the alleyway. The body was far heavier than she had anticipated, and the pain that had seized both her hands did not make things any easier. Even the man's blood seemed to be working against her. There was far more of the crimson liquid than she had anticipated, and this only worked to make it harder to maintain her grip on the body. It took well over the planned five minutes to drag the corpse to where her car lay parked, and by then she was caked in blood as well as sweat.

She paused to catch her breath for a moment before unlocking the trunk of the minivan, but that's when she felt a light buzzing coming from the right pocket of her suit pants. Desperate to keep up appearances, and not give anyone an ounce of suspicion as to what she was truly doing, she frantically dug into her pocket to pull the cellphone free. By the time she had done so, her lock screen showed she had one missed call from her husband. An audible grunt of frustration escaped from the back of her throat, but she took a moment to calm herself before calling right back.

"Hey honey," Jonathan answered with just a tiny hint of worry in his voice, "are you okay?"

Jenelle knew she had indirectly done this to herself. She always answered Jonathan's calls, so missing just one of them would raise some concern. Of course, her husband was so sweet that he would only be worried about her safety. She could tell from his voice as well as all the years of having been with him that the idea of her doing something nefarious never passed through his mind when she didn't answer right away. If she could play this with just a little skill, everything would be fine … at least with her family.

"Yeah, I'm fine. I just got held up at work," she paused for a moment then added, "I'm just leaving right now, so that's probably why I missed your call. You know my phone doesn't work well when I'm taking elevators."

"Damn! I'm sorry you had to work so late. They're having you stay almost two hours later than usual. That's not right," Jonathan said with some aggravation in his voice. "I'd really like to talk to your boss, one on one, and give him a piece of my mind."

Jenelle smiled. She had successfully diverted her husband's attention, so he wasn't even focused on her tardiness. It seemed like she had adverted catastrophe but a sudden shout coming from one of the entrances to the alley broke her confidence. She looked to find a dirty man in ragged clothing stumbling his way over the worn-down cement, heading toward her. There was an angry look on his face and he had a rather large glass bottle gripped in his right hand.

"You did it, lady! It was you!" the man shouted. "I seen you do it, you damn bitch."

Jenelle felt a twinge of panic grip her heart, not because of the homeless man himself, he was no real threat or danger, but because of what he was doing. His yelling, all that noise, it would no doubt eventually draw attention from somewhere. The last thing she needed was to have someone else venturing into the alleyway and discovering her grizzly work. So, she drowned out her husband's voice on the phone and slammed the trunk of the van with more force than was necessary. The homeless man continued his staggered advance toward her, screaming obscenities and gibberish as he went. She scrambled around to the front of her vehicle and got inside where she struggled to locate her keys. Her eyes glanced at the rearview mirror to spot the intoxicated beggar drawing ever closer. Finally, she found her keys and shoved them into the ignition. As her car roared to life, she flipped the drunkard the bird and sped out of the alleyway.

"Hey, are you listening to me?" Jonathan asked as his voice suddenly came back into focus for Jenelle.

She was about to reply as she glanced at her rearview mirror just to make sure no one was following her. It took her by complete surprise to see the visage of the well-dressed man glaring at her while most of his body remained cloaked in eternal shadow.

"I'm uh … I'm sorry, honey … I … couldn't find my keys. I had a mini-panic attack there for a second. What were you saying?" she asked.

There came a long pause from the other end before Jonathan lightly inquired, "Is everything okay? You sound really stressed out."

Thanks to her rearview mirror, Jenelle was able to lock eyes with the imposing being sitting in her backseat, oozing its intimidating aura into every fiber of her car. With her attention divided between two things, she didn't notice her fingers slipping from the steering wheel. Thanks to her hands being slick with blood she very nearly lost control of the vehicle. In a panic, she readjusted her grip with a sudden yank which caused the vehicle to swerve. Narrowly, the car avoided colliding with the one that was driving in the lane next to it. She heard a loud honk from the irate driver of the other vehicle but ignored it.

"It was just a long day at work, babe. I'm pretty exhausted, that's all," she said, finally replying to her husband with as much fatigue in her tone as she could muster.

Jonathan responded with a frustrated sigh, "I can't believe they had you working that late. They know you have kids to pick up."

A sudden wave of panic gripped hold of Jenelle as she stared at her blood-covered hands. The kids. She hadn't picked up the kids. Well … she couldn't. Not with a dead body in the car. What the hell was she supposed to do?

"Don't worry honey, I'll go pick up the kiddos," Jonathan spoke up as if reading her mind.

"Really?" she exclaimed, pleasantly surprised.

"Of course, you've had a hell of a day," he paused, "though I do need you to do one thing for me."

Jenelle hesitated as she once again made eye contact with the powerful entity in her backseat. "Okay, what is it?"

"Can you run by the store and pick up some celery and chicken stock? I need those before I can start on the soup for dinner."

"Sure. Sure, I can do that. No problem."

"Awesome! Thanks, baby. I'll see you in a bit. Love you!"

"Love you too," Jenelle responded the second before she ended the call. She picked up on a sudden intensity that filled the shadowed man's eyes and knew she had to address it. "I'll be picking up the groceries …" she sucked in a large breath then added, "after I take care of this body."

The power being showed its approval with a simple nod, letting her know she had appeased it for now. She furiously racked her brain for secluded spots near where she currently was as she drove on. Jonathan would be expecting her somewhat soonish. Traffic would only cover for some level of tardiness. She had to find a place where she could take care of her dinner first, and then she could focus on picking up the stuff for soup.

THIRTEEN
DIARY ENTRY: NOVEMBER 3RD, 1952

It was all a clever ploy. Just like all the other men I have ever known, my mysterious benefactor only wanted to use me. Sure, it was for something completely different from the others, but the result is still the same. How foolish of me to fall for it so easily. Perhaps I will chalk it up to a combination of my young age when he first came to me and the unpleasantness of my situation at the time. Those two factors certainly had something to do with it, but with my advanced years those things no longer hold sway. I can see his motive as clear as day and it does not bode well for me.

For now, I am still of use to him, or rather ... it. Thanks to time and the number of our encounters I have realized that the man is just an illusion, a way to hide the true form of my supposed benefactor. Each time it visits there is more of it hidden in shadow. Or perhaps, it is revealing more of itself to me and my eyes cannot comprehend what they are being shown. Either way, it allows me to live for now. I am sure I will have plenty of life left to live, but I must be always ready to serve.

There's no mistaking it, its patience with me has worn. Not to a point beyond where it can be mended, but I would rather not test this being any further. I have been granted power beyond any mortal person, but not enough strength to free myself from its control. It's a brilliant ploy and one I had fallen for wholeheartedly until recently. How foolish I was to think that I could one day escape its grasp. That time will never come. I am a servant for the rest of my days, but that is not so bad. The gift of enduring youth has been granted to me, being a glorified errand boy for such a treasure is just a minor price to pay.

Though I am grateful for what I have been given, I know that I deserve more. I have carried out the wordless orders of this ... this thing for decades now. Besides a minor hiccup here or there, I have done what has been asked without question and to perfection. Yet, the power bestowed upon me has continued to dwindle. Despite the strength that I have been given, I can still feel the unrelenting call of age. My body is withering, I can feel it. Granted, much slower than those around me, but I can feel my flesh begin to degrade.

It took over sixty years, but the first wrinkles are beginning to creep onto my face. My hairs are greying, though there remains plenty of color in them. Even worse, the aches I feel in my body are no longer the calls of my master, they are from old age. The pops and cracks I hear moving about during the day are constant reminders that I am not immortal, unlike the thing that holds dominion over me. But that is not fair! I have served. Should I not be granted immortality for such obedience?

Perhaps I have actually been granted eternal life, but a twisted form of it. My benefactor will not allow me to die as long as I dispatch the targets it chooses, but that doesn't mean I get to remain in a youthful state as well. Of course! This is the true price of immortality. I will be allowed to live an unnaturally long life, but everything around me, including myself, will continue to degrade. How cruel. This body will continue to wither even though the rest of me shall remain intact. Very well, I shall abide by these terrible conditions. Though, I suppose I don't have any choice in the matter. It is either I die at the hand of this inhuman thing now or sometime far down the road. I choose far from now, and based on how slowly I am aging, it will be far from now. At least I can take solace in that.

However, it seems that the rest of my family will not take my master up on its offer. I know it has gone to each of them, and they have all rebuffed its gifts. Fools. I thought I raised them better, but it seems not. Even in my frustration with the deal I have been given, it is clear I have made the right decision in accepting its offer. Clearly, you take as many years as you possibly can get, and that was what was offered to them. And that is why my eldest is six feet under right now while I remain above the dirt. The doctors can say it was a heart attack that killed him, but I know the truth. A foolish decision and my master's wrath are what killed my son.

Even my youngest made the wrong choice. I can see it on her face. The deep wrinkles that have begun to form around her eyes as well as the occasional groan of pain tell me everything I need to know. She honestly looks older than me, and even more so with each passing day. Is this just another way for it to keep me in line? It is showing me what would have happened if I hadn't taken its offer. It is the most vindictive way to do so, but I must admit it is effective. I shall serve it and prolong my life. Ultimately, nothing else matters except making sure that I continue to live, no matter what. Even as this body rots away.

FOURTEEN

UNLIKE HER MOTHER

Jenelle hesitated as her hand gripped tightly around the handle of the hospital door. She knew she had to enter eventually, but there was a dread that kept her from doing so. Her mother had always been so strong and lively, she was frightened to see the state that such an incredible person had been reduced to. An arc of pain stabbed the back of her neck causing a muscle spasm that jerked her hand, and in turn, the door handle. This created a fairly loud sound that she had no doubt her mother had heard. Now her presence was known, which meant she couldn't stand still outside the room.

With a long exhale to buy her just a few more seconds in the hallway, she finally pushed open the door. Immediately, she was assailed by the smell of death. It was a scent she had become accustomed to since beginning her gruesome partnership with the otherworldly man. Each of her victims reeked of the odor just before their lives were extinguished, but this time it smelled different. It was not as pronounced as the other times she had encountered it. The scent was duller and packed less power behind it, most likely because her mother's situation was different from one of the people she had slaughtered. They had been killed off quickly, while her mother was made to suffer.

"Hey, you finally made it," a weak voice called out from across the room.

Jenelle's gaze fell on the lone bed and the sickly figure lying in it. Her stomach twisted into knots as she approached the bed. With each step, she was able to make out more of the details of her mother and how dire her condition was. Just a few months ago, her mom was perfectly healthy, her body still in pretty good condition. Now, it had been reduced to nothing more than a withering husk with skin nearly devoid of all color. It hurt so much to see her mother reduced to a fraction of her former self. She came to a stop on the right side of the bed and continued to study the sickly woman before her, while some of her focus was diverted to preventing tears from welling up. After nearly a minute spent in stillness, Jenelle leaned down and planted a gentle kiss on her mother's forehead.

"Of course I made it," she softly replied, finally responding to the initial comment.

Laurie managed to muster a weak smile as she whispered, "I just haven't seen you in so long."

"I know, I ..." Jenelle began, ready to list off all the things she had been busy with, but then she made eye contact with her mom and all those excuses all of a sudden seemed so pathetic. She sunk down in the chair just a few feet from the bed and admitted, "I know I haven't been around a lot ... or at all ... and I'm sorry."

"Hey, I get it. You've been busy with college. That's the whole point, you know. You're supposed to be busy. If you weren't, you probably wouldn't be doing it right."

Jenelle furiously shook her head. "No, that's no excuse. For fuck's sake Mom, you're dying of cancer ..."

"Language," Laurie interjected before wincing in pain.

Upon witnessing the pain her mother was experiencing,

Jenelle fell silent as the sensation of guilt festered in her gut. This left the room in silence besides the rhythmic beeping of the heart monitor tucked away in the corner. Eventually, she couldn't stand the awkward feeling that hung in the air and cut through it by asking, "So, how are you feeling?"

"Well, besides the cancer everything is pretty peachy," Laurie replied with a wry smile.

"Mom, can you … can you not joke for just a little bit?" Jenelle pleaded with a hint of annoyance in her voice.

Laurie stretched her arm out and gently placed a hand on top of her daughter's. "Comedy is how I'm able to get through all of this. Hospitals on their own suck the life out of me, but being stuck in one is making things so miserable."

"I get it. I just … I want to be serious for a little bit. Only a little bit. Is that okay?" When her mother responded with a nod, Jenelle let out a small sigh of relief. "Good. Now, really, how are you feeling?"

"Truthfully, I feel like shit," she let out a weak chuckle. "I wish I didn't have to say it like that, but there's really no other way to describe it."

Jenelle scanned her mother's frame, and though it was mostly hidden under a thin blanket, she could easily spot the significant weight loss. From just a guess, she estimated that her mom had lost at least forty pounds. It was clear that things were not going well, and if things didn't get better soon, she would have a funeral to attend. Yet, she held on to a glimmer of hope that maybe things weren't as dire as they seemed from mere appearances.

"How's it going, with the treatment and everything? Is it working?"

Laurie gave a small nod. "The doctors seem to think so. Though, at this point, I think it's all about prolonging the inevitable."

Her mother's words stunned Jenelle. It felt like an incredible weight had fallen on top of her and there was nothing she could do but be crushed by it. There was nothing definitive in what Laurie had said, but she could infer, though she chose not to accept the obvious truth.

She was completely overwhelmed with dread, and her mind couldn't focus as she tried to speak. "What? W-What do you mean? Prolong? Prolong what? Is … I … is something … what is happening?"

The meek smile finally left her mother's face, gently morphing into a frown. With a look of sad realization, she responded to her daughter, "Your father didn't tell you, did he?"

"He said you had cancer, and that it was bad. But it was treatable. That's … that's what he said." She looked up, locking eyes with her mother. "They're treating it, aren't they? You're going to beat this, right?"

"Honey …" Laurie shook her head, "it's stage four. There's no coming back from this."

Unable to fully process what she had just been told; Jenelle sat there in stunned silence. She tried to form a complete sentence, but instead, all that came out was, "It can't …"

"Hey, I'm almost fifty. For a Dayten, that's a long time to be alive," Laurie tried to comfort her daughter. "I've lived a good life. There's nothing wrong with leaving it earlier than expected."

Jenelle stood up, shaking her head. Her breathing was fast and irregular. "No. This can't be happening." She placed her hands on the top of her head and started to pace by the bed. "This is impossible, you were fine just a few months ago. How could this happen?"

A sudden pain shooting through the back of her neck brought her to a standstill. She grasped at the afflicted body part while letting out an audible grunt of pain.

"Are you all right?" Laurie asked with concern.

Jenelle felt a powerful aura fill the air and she shot her focus toward an empty corner of the room. Suddenly, the silent stranger appeared, wearing the same outdated clothes as he always did. However, part of his left leg was missing, or rather, it was covered in some type of shadow that made it invisible to the naked eye.

"You're behind this," Jenelle whispered through clenched teeth.

"What? What are you saying?" Laurie asked in confusion. "Are you okay? Should I call a nurse?"

The silent man responded to Jenelle's question, not with a nod or shake of his head, but by flashing a closed-lip smile. Rage morphed around her denial and she turned her gaze away from the man. She looked at her mother in her withered state and an idea fired across her brain.

"This doesn't have to be it," Jenelle said as she gripped the footboard at the end of the bed to help take some of the focus off the agony ripping through the back of her neck. "There's a way to beat the cancer."

Laurie shook her head, "Drawing it out with some expensive treatment isn't going to …"

"It's not a treatment. It's a cure!" Jenelle insisted at a volume that was almost a yell. She noticed her mother react with surprise, and lowered her voice a bit. "What if I told you there was a cure? You could get rid of the cancer for good. All you had to do was one thing. Would you do it?"

There was a growing look of concern on Laurie's face as she slowly replied, "I guess I would. Though it would really depend on that one thing."

"Really? You wouldn't just do it?" Jenelle replied with genuine surprise.

"Well, in this hypothetical s-"

"It's not a hypothetical!" Jenelle snapped. She shook her head. "Pretend it's not a hypothetical. This thing could cure you of your cancer. Would you do it?"

"It would depend on what I have to do," Laurie replied, sticking to her original answer.

Jenelle shot a glance at the silent stranger to see that his smile had turned back to the normal emotionless expression that he wore. "What does it matter what the thing is?" she asked in frustration.

"Because everything has a price. Nothing is free."

"The price is that you got cancer, Mom!" Jenelle exclaimed in irritation as she white-knuckled the footboard.

Laurie shook her head. "No, I have cancer. That's something that just happened. It's a part of nature. There's nothing you can do to stop it. But in your scenario, you're saying there's a way to cure it. The cure is what's being hawked, and the price for it has yet to be paid."

It took a moment for Jenelle to digest what had been said but once it had, she knew there was no convincing her mom of taking the unspoken deal. She turned to the silent stranger, and as a final Hail Mary asked, "Could I do it for her?"

"W-Who are you talking to?"

Jenelle ignored her mother and focused on the silent man who simply shook his head. "Why not? She needs this. You never came to her like you did to me."

The stranger continued to shake his head until something suddenly clicked in Jenelle's brain. A memory of her mom lying in bed, groaning from intense back pain. Then a dozen more moments of her mother dealing with pain flooded her mind all at once. Some of them were her own, but others were being shown to her by the silent man. All the painful moments that Laurie endured, ran through her thoughts and delivered a realization that astonished her.

"You didn't accept it," she said turning to face her mother. "I don't know if you fully understood what was being offered, or you just didn't think it through, but you rejected it."

Confusion mixed with Laurie's concern as she responded,

"Honey, are you sure you're okay? You're not making any sense."

"The man in the strange clothes, when did you see him?" Jenelle demanded to know.

"What? What man?"

"The silent one who always feels out of place. The one who offered you the gift of no pain. When did he come to you!"

Laurie shook her head, "No pain? I-I don't understand. What are you trying to say?"

"It makes sense now. All those times you were hobbled in bed and could barely move. I remember your groans of agony. Your pleas for the pain to end. It makes sense now," Jenelle said as she reached up and squeezed the back of her neck in hopes of decreasing the unpleasant sensation surging through it. "I understand not accepting the offer when it was just you. I'm sure you thought you didn't need it, that you could muscle your way through the misery, but what about when you finally had a family? Did it ever occur to you to do it for us? For me?"

The concern finally shifted to fear and Laurie grasped for the call button. She pressed it while saying, "I don't know what's wrong, honey, but I'm getting you some help right now. Just please try to calm down."

"Why should I?" Jenelle snapped. "You can live! You have a chance to live and stay here with Dad and me, but you won't take it! And why? Because of some stupid code of ethics?"

Laurie did not respond with any words, she just kept pressing the call button. Jenelle stopped her rant just long enough to see the fear in her mother's eyes. Terror that was there, not because of a life-threatening illness or a cosmic being with immense power, but because her daughter was acting erratic. This softened the anger Jenelle had been feeling and a twinge of regret started to seep into her heart. A stab of pain in the back of her neck quickly put an end to that and she audibly gasped from it.

She staggered toward the door of the room while barely getting out, "I'm sorry. I forgot I have to do something."

"Wait! Don't go anywhere!" Laurie called out after her daughter. "You're not well!"

Jenelle pushed open the door and stumbled into the hallway where she fumbled her way to the nearest elevator while clutching her neck. Surprisingly, no one said anything despite the pained expression plastered across her face. She was able to get on the elevator without being accosted, and left the floor before a nurse even reached her mother's room. Once the doors opened, she forced her body to push through the pain until she collapsed into a chair in the cafeteria. There she sat, thinking about the difference between her and her mother's decisions.

Why was her mom being so stubborn? If you were in intense pain and there was something that could stop it, why would you not say yes? It didn't make sense to cling to some misplaced morality if it meant you died. And what about Jenelle? Her mom was choosing to leave her without a mother. That was selfish, plain and simple. Not only was her mom making the wrong decision, but one that hurt everyone around her too. As she continued to stew in her anger, Jenelle glanced at the area around her until she stopped on a random man filling up his tray with some food. His back was turned to her so she could easily spot the violet glow that emanated from the top of his spine.

It was at that moment that Jenelle decided to always do what was best for loved ones, by doing what was best for herself. After all, the people close to her would be hurt far more if she died early than anything else. She stood up slowly as the pain in her neck subsided for a moment, then sauntered over toward the unsuspecting man with the faint shine.

FIFTEEN
FOR THE CHILDREN

Jenelle bit into the unidentified organ, ripping away a huge chunk of it. She chewed the fatty piece of meat while the sweet flavor that had been placed on it through supernatural means covered her tastebuds. Even with the potent taste holding the true unpleasantness of the situation at bay, there were still moments when the flavor of blood would seep through. Though truth be told, she strangely didn't mind those moments. She had begun to associate the metallic taste with the easement of pain and the pleasurable feeling of gaining strength. The overall experience was still horrific, but she had done it enough times that it didn't seem as monstrous anymore.

She tore off another piece of flesh with her teeth and checked to see how much of the organ remained. It seemed that only a few bites worth of meat were left, and she hoped that would be enough. Jenelle turned away from the carved-up body and expected to see the well-dressed man waiting for her, but he wasn't there. In surprise, she stood up and scanned the dingy alleyway looking for him. Her gaze eventually fell on her car, which was facing away from her, and there she spotted the stranger sitting in it, his back to her. In a panic, she took off in a dead sprint toward the vehicle, reaching it in a matter of seconds. She threw open the car door, coming to a stop only a few inches from him.

In as forceful a tone as she could muster, she growled, "Get away from him."

The well-dressed man turned his attention away from Jenelle's infant son, strapped in his baby carrier while fast asleep, and stared at her. He responded to the clearly hostile tone by raising a questioning eyebrow.

"You stay away from him. You can't have him," Jenelle commanded. She pointed a finger directly in the well-dressed man's face. "I won't let you."

She was completely taken by surprise when he responded, speaking for the first time that she had heard him do so. He said only one word, but it hit her with a massive wave of dread as he whispered, "Someday."

In an instant, the man disappeared from in front of her, throwing her off her guard. That made it even more jarring when his voice came from behind her, whispering one more time, "Someday."

All-encompassing terror froze Jenelle in place, and she dared not turn around for fear of what she would see. Instead, she stared at some random spot in her car and waited for the feeling of something being directly behind her to disappear. A few, unnaturally long moments passed before she stopped feeling the sensation, but she remained frozen for a couple more seconds just to be sure. Slowly, she lifted her hands where she could see them. She stared at the crimson that stained them, not daring to focus on anything else. Another minute or so passed before she heard the familiar sound of a cosmic being absorbing a corpse into its essence. The blood that covered her hands vanished and she was finally left with silence. She let out the breath she didn't even realize she had been holding and gasped for air. Once oxygen was flowing through her lungs, she scrambled into the car to check on her infant child, who to her relief, seemed perfectly fine. He hadn't even woken up from his nap.

"That man won't ever take you from me," she whispered to her sleeping baby. "Mommy won't ever let that happen. I'm only doing things for that bad man so I can be here while you grow up."

It was the same justification she had given for her actions when her mother died in the hospital nearly a decade ago. Jenelle wasn't doing this for herself; it was for her family. Her husband and her son, as well as all the people she was close to. She was preventing heartache by prolonging her life. The sacrifice of a person every year or so was well worth it to her to keep her loved ones from mourning. Though, subconsciously, she knew why she was really doing it. She wouldn't face the truth and admit to herself that she was murdering people so she could extend her own life. It was that simple. There was no altruistic intention behind it, but facing that reality was more gruesome for her than what she did to her victim's bodies.

"I'm doing this for you," she whispered to her sleeping son. It was a lie, but it gave her comfort. "I'm doing this for you."

SIXTEEN

THE NEXT GENERATION

imon checked his phone once again and frowned. His mother hadn't texted him back yet, which was a bit concerning. Normally, she did so within a few minutes, but there had been no response since last night. He tried to shrug it off and went back to staring at the barely typed paper that sat open on his computer. The coffee shop buzzed with people and sounds, but that was not what kept him from progressing in his work report. He was a little worried about his mom, but more than that there was an ache that sent an unpleasant tingle through his hands. Each time he tried to type something his fingers would erupt with waves of pain.

At first, he thought he could ignore the discomfort and it would go away, but several days had gone by with no signs of it stopping. For a bit, he thought he had some early form of arthritis, but that didn't make any sense. He was far too young to have such an ailment, and he didn't do anything that would cause such damage to his hands. However, the most concerning thing was that the pain seemed to be getting worse. Even when compared to the day before, Simon could tell the aches had gotten more intense. The pain hindered his ability to do his job, as well as carry out menial tasks. He hadn't been able to go to the gym since the unpleasant sensations started because he couldn't lift any weights without feeling waves of agony. Simon hated to admit it, especially after wasting time coming to a café to see if that would help, but he had a serious problem.

He was just about to call it quits and power down his laptop when he felt like someone was standing a little too close to him. Instinctively, he glanced up from his computer screen to see a man standing on the opposite side of the small table he was seated at, less than arm's length from him. The stranger wore what looked to be some very outdated dress clothes that were definitely out of place in the coffee shop. Adding another level to the weirdness of the man, he was staring right at Simon. The two made eye contact for the briefest of moments before Simon looked back at his computer screen. He didn't want to cause a scene, but if that weirdo continued to stare at him, he was going to get confrontational.

He took in a deep breath and readied to start shouting, but when he glanced back up the strange man was gone. There was a feeling of relief that washed over him but that was rudely interrupted by the unwelcomed pain stretching out through his fingers. He quickly gathered up his things and headed for the exit, but as he reached the door something caught his attention out of the corner of his eye. The strange man was standing just a few feet away from him on his left side. Simon glanced over at the spot where he was sure the stranger had been standing but found nothing except for two trashcans waiting for him. He pushed open the door and left the café, cradling his hands in one another as he left. Meanwhile, the well-dressed man watched from across the street and eagerly awaited the right moment to show Simon his first victim.

The End

ABOUT THE AUTHOR

 **Radar DeBoard** is just a simple horror writer, living in the bleak state of Kansas. Recently, he has grown weary of the limitations of his craft when it comes to scares. Sure, he has terrified many thanks to having seven published books to his name as well as being featured in dozens of horror anthologies, but the fear from those stories wears off. He wishes to create something so horrific that it lingers in the reader's mind for years to come. Creating something of such unfathomable terror would cement him in the brains of those who purchase his books.

Plus, it would be like he left a piece of himself in each copy of his work. A small bit of himself that can grow and watch, waiting for the right time to deliver a final fright.

A NOTE FROM TRUBORN PRESS

We want to thank our readers for their support and enthusiasm. Your passion for stories fuels our commitment to bring you the horror that is strange and horrifying in the best of ways.

We appreciate any and all reviews, so help us out by leaving your thoughts online.

Thank you again for spending your time with us and remember to...

Follow us everywhere: @trubornpress
Subscribe to our newsletter today!
www.trubornpress.com

CONTENT NOTES

- Death
- Gore
- Sexual assault (attempted)
- Murder
- Drugging
- Child endangerment
- Strong language
- Supernatural themes

www.ingramcontent.com/pod-product-compliance
Lightning Source LLC
Chambersburg PA
CBHW030011010826
48973CB00009B/2752